Galaxy Lessons

By Harlowe Frost

ISBN eBook: 978-1-959981-51-0
ISBN paperback: 978-1-959981-52-7

Editor: Weslee Imrisek
Developmental Editor: Angela Grimes
Cover Art: Getcovers.com
Formatting: Huckleberry Rahr

Books In the Magic Of The Galaxy Series

Series 1: Viera Kor

Book 1: Galaxy Lessons

Book 2: Magic Lessons

Book 3: Conflict Lessens

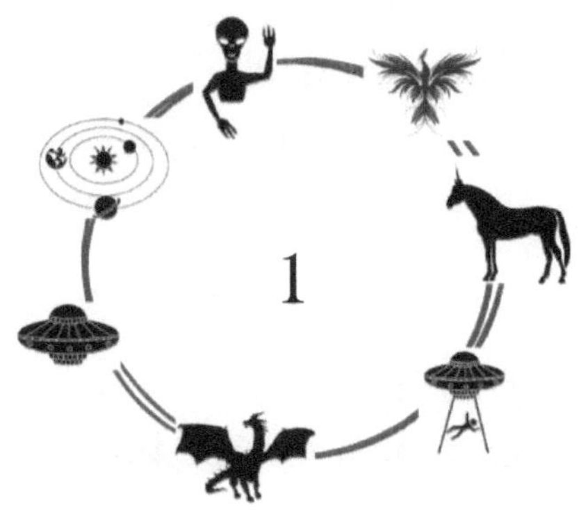

Best Teacher In The Galaxy

Viera

Viera sat at her desk and gazed around her classroom. She looked at her watch—three forty-five—so close to quitting time. Her left earbud sat snug in her ear playing a selection of nineties alternative rock. Currently, *Green Day* wailed. She got up and danced around her room, tidying up.

Her phone buzzed, cutting through the music. Checking her watch, Viera saw 'Dork-Face,' her best friend since college. Smiling, she tapped the plastic in her ear. "Betsy! I thought you were busy today. Is something wrong?"

There was a pause. "Any kids with you?"

"No! Thank goodness. My room is clean and clear ... of kids, that is. I'm clearing away all their detritus. Then I'm heading home for a week of relaxation. We're on for Tuesday right? Girls' night out? My staycation needs some fun."

"Um." Betsy sounded distracted. "What? Yeah, Tuesday. We're totally going out."

"Is something up? Spill." Viera groused, "Why did you call when you're clearly distracted?"

Betsy chuckled. "Astute as always, my friend. I'm just trying to finish up this job. I thought we could get together tonight and wanted to check in with you before you got yourself a hot date with that mom you're always going on about."

"Scout's mom, Thorn?" Viera blushed. "I mean, what? There's no 'mom.' Not only would it be inappropriate, it's ... just no."

"You'll only be Scout's teacher for a few more weeks, then you're free to do whatever you want."

She could hear the smile in Betsy's voice. "However, we should find you someone on Tuesday."

Viera dropped into her chair, the only comfortable one in the room. "Right ... a date. Find someone who wants to date a messy second-grade teacher who frequently talks like a half-wit."

"Just because you know more about the latest cartoon than the popular drama on TV doesn't make you less intelligent, it makes you good at your job. Now, stop pouting. When do you get out of there?"

"Soon. I mean, I could leave now, but I plan on forgetting as much as I can this week, so I want to make sure when I walk in at seven a.m. a week from Monday that everything is ready to go, because you know those kiddos will be off and running."

Viera dragged her body out of the chair. What was the point of hands-free if she didn't use her hands while she spoke? "Speaking of ready to go, I'd better get moving on the clean-up."

"Good," Betsy said. "So, tonight? Mexican and margaritas?"

She wanted to swoon. "I can't. Not tonight, I'm busy. I promised Mother I'd go on a blind date ...

again." As annoyed as the date made her, the tables all cleaned and in line brought a level of peace to her.

"Your ... Mother? Is it with a guy or a gal?"

"Stop!" Viera snapped, exasperated. She put the last of the books onto the bookshelf. "I'll fight with my parents when we're face to face. We've discussed this before."

Betsy snorted. "You haven't left Wisconsin since you moved here for college. The likelihood of you visiting Florida or your parents coming here are next to zero. I've never met a group of people who travels less. You and your family could win a prize for staying within their sphere of comfort."

Viera harrumphed. "I travel!"

"Leaving the greater Madison area to go to the Milwaukee museums doesn't count." There was a pause. "Chicago doesn't count either. It's less than three hours away, different state or not."

"*You* take a bunch of second graders to Chicago on an air-conditioned school bus. It's like walking to Mordor."

Viera turned in place. *I think I've gotten it all. I may be free to go!* "Fine, I'll dedicate a couple of days of spring break to drive north for more than three hours, deal?"

Betsy chuckled. "Deal. Look, I have to go. A client is ... well, their son wandered off. I'm going to do a quick drive around their neighborhood. He's probably at the playground." Such a strange job Betsy had, being a P.I. One day investigating if a husband was cheating, the next, finding a missing kid.

"You're on the job and you called me instead?"

"Nah, they just texted me. I'm better than that. Tuesday, my friend."

"Tuesday!" Viera pocketed her phone and sat, making sure that when she sat on Monday, everything would *feel* correct.

"Ms. Kor! Ms. Kor! Are you still here? Ms. Kor!" A small boy with brown hair and brown eyes bounded into her room. Young Scout was one of her favorite students—and not because his mom had enchanted her with her jewel-like green eyes and auburn hair—it was his utter innocence. Every time they learned something new, Scout vibrated with excitement, wanting to know everything. He was always the first to ask questions.

A smile stretched across her face. "Afternoon, Scout. What are you doing back in class? You should've been long gone."

It was almost half past four and she was ready to go home and be done with teaching for a whole week. She knew he should've been home almost an hour ago. He didn't live far, and she was pretty sure his mom picked him up. A small smile crossed her face at the thought of his mom.

"I got home and remembered the present I got you. I forgot to give it to you, and I wanted you to have it before spring break."

"You have a gift? For me?" Viera smiled down at the boy. It was so sweet of him to have gotten her something. *I love working with kids this age.*

He reached into a sack he carried with him and pulled out a slightly battered box. The paper covering the package had small unicorns and rainbows on it.

"This paper is lovely."

Scout snorted. "It's funny, isn't it?"

Viera smiled at him. "It's very colorful, and I like unicorns."

A bright smile on his face, he handed it up to her. This was the smile that always melted her heart.

The other students teased him for his awkwardness, but she found the boy utterly endearing.

"Thank you, Scout." She took the gift and carefully removed the wrapping from the box. Lifting the cardboard top, she found a navy-blue mug with white stars. In gold lettering it proclaimed: *Best Teacher In The Galaxy!!!* She laughed. "All the galaxy, huh? You know that for a fact?"

"I do!" he pronounced with conviction.

"Thank you. Come here and give me a hug, sweetie." She placed the mug on her desk and engulfed him in a hug. Squeezing him, she sighed. "You need to get home. Your mom's probably worried." *Should I walk him home? I could see his mom then. No, it's not about me, it's about him.*

He pulled back but stayed in the circle of her arms. "It's okay, I left a note."

"You sure?" Viera checked her watch before placing her hand around his back. "It's four-thirty. Maybe I should give her a call."

His eyes widened as his body stiffened. The room started to sparkle and twist. Then the walls seemed to melt. *Holy cow, what is going on? Is it something I ate? Fumes from the white board markers?* Terrified, she squeezed the boy to her, unsure what was going on.

From below her chin where he was squished to her chest, his voice came out muffled. "It's four-thirty? Oh, no ... I'm sorry, Ms. Kor. I'm really sorry."

Not In Kansas

Viera

Viera's chair evaporated from under her butt, and she collapsed to the floor with a yelp. Still holding Scout, she took the poor boy with her. He squealed as if he were on a rollercoaster, then tumbled away.

She threw her hands back to stop her fall. Mouth gaping open, she took in her surroundings.

The room was small with a tightly-made bed, a dresser, and a few toys in a box in the corner. A well-loved looking bookcase stood near a small bean bag with a lamp next to it. Its laden shelves groaned under the weight of books stacked on and around it.

Did we just teleport?—transport? beam?—to Scout's house? Is this his bedroom?

Scout leapt to his feet. "I'm sorry, Ms. Kor ... um ... welcome to my room?" His face scrunched up in an amused question.

The lighting was bright but seemed natural instead of artificial. Viera swung her head, looking for a window. *Does he keep his blinds closed? That's odd. Scout loves playing outside. He seems to want to go outside whenever there's a chance, even in winter.*

Her eyes passed over a *Star Wars* poster on the wall of the stars going into hyperspace, the bright lights zooming by the windshield. *Great movie, kid ... classic!*

Once she'd gone full circle, her brows came together. *Doesn't he have a window?* Then it dawned on her. She snapped her gaze back to the movie poster ... the *not* movie poster.

"Scout, where are we?"

He slapped his hands over his mouth. "We're in my room! Isn't it great?" He sounded a bit wild.

He bit his lip, eyes wide. "I'm going to be in so much trouble."

"Scout Firoza, where did you get to? Do you know how many people ..." The door opened and a turquoise—woman? alien?—with stormy green eyes and a royal purple high ponytail burst in. She wore jeans and a light blue button-down.

Is that an alien? Am I in danger? Where am I? Is she wearing Earth clothing? What the fuck?

The alien's mouth gaped open as she gazed at Viera. After a quick audible breath, she smiled. "Ms. Kor, this is unexpected."

Viera thought her head may explode. *Did she just call me by name?* She tried to get the tornado of thoughts to slow down into a semblance of sense and words. "Ya ... ya ..." She hated how airy her breath sounded. *Get it together woman!* "Ya know me?" Her voice raised more at the end than the question deserved, and why couldn't she say full words?

The alien sighed, then the skin shimmered and became a sun-kissed human with tan skin. Her vivid purple hair shifted to a deep auburn, and it clicked.

Viera felt like she'd been kicked in the gut. "Ms. Firoza? Is that you?" *Of course it's her. She's standing right there. Even with turquoise skin and purple hair she didn't look that different.*

A soft smile spread on the woman's face. "You okay?"

Am I? Viera pushed herself up to standing. She knew she wouldn't be okay if she stayed sitting on her ass on Scout's floor. "Yes? Well, no. You're an alien ... who can change colors. And I'm ... not on Earth?" Again, her voice had a mind of its own.

"Okay, you seem to be doing good so far. I've seen humans who've done much worse at learning about the reality of aliens." There was a sparkle to Ms. Firoza's eyes.

Viera tried to moisten her dry mouth, but it wasn't going to happen. "Am I? I don't feel like I'm doing a good job. Do many humans know? What was the worst reaction?"

Ms. Firoza's shoulders dropped as she came over and took Viera's hand and led her to Scout's bed. A small spark of excitement tingled through her body.

Stop it, body. When she was human that was one thing ... but she turns blue! What if she can turn into a chair or a dog! Gah!

They sat and Ms. Firoza rested her hand on Viera's knee. Viera ignored the sensations that touch caused as the *alien* spoke. "Some scream, some deny what they see, and some get violent. Not many know, though, as you probably could've guessed. When my people came to your planet, we made sure to check in with those in charge."

"Take me to your leader," Viera intoned in a robotic voice.

Ms. Firoza chuckled. "Exactly."

"Okay, so, questions." She licked her lips. "Ms. Firoza, how long have you been on Earth, and why are you leaving? And can you take me back? I have things I need to do." Viera checked her watch. It was almost five. Her date was at seven; she had time. She gazed up, thinking about how much she had to do at home before the date, her eyes landing on the perfect ponytail.

The hair started waving back and forth as Ms. Firoza shook her head. "Can we start with you calling me Thorn, especially when not in front of the crew? It seems silly to be so formal. If it's okay, I'll call you Viera?"

Viera nodded. "Sounds like a deal."

Scout snorted. "I'm sticking with Ms. Kor until the school year's over." He crossed his arms over his chest.

Viera smiled, warmth blooming within her.

Thorn continued. "I'm sorry, no, I can't take you back home. We are on a tight deadline. It's a two-day trip to get to the summit. I'm the acting leader for my people, the chanzii. I can't be late. It's a three-day meeting, then two days back, just in time for Scout to return to school. His education and socialization are very important to us."

"You're kidnapping me?" Her heart pounded like a snare drum. "I can't go home?"

"You're not a prisoner. We'll show you and teach you about the ship, the space station, and the different races. Scout loves your class because you enjoy learning new things as much as he does. But we can't take you back to Earth yet. Not until our planned return. Finding Scout already put us behind."

Viera sat frozen on the bed. She gazed across the room towards a door which must lead to Scout's closet but didn't really see much. Her mind was a maelstrom of thoughts. *I wanted a staycation to get away from the day-to-day of my life ... but now I'm really getting away. When I decided to get away, I didn't mean off the fucking planet Earth! Thorn is an alien ... a fucking alien.*

As if struck by lightning, she slowly turned to contemplate Scout, who stood in the center of his room, following the conversation. "What is your natural form?"

The boy giggled. His body shifted and, like his mother, he had turquoise skin and dark purple hair. He swung his arms out with a wide grin. "Ta-da!"

She couldn't help but smile at his exuberance. "Does it feel better to be like that?"

He shrugged. "Once I change to the Earth colors, it's easy to maintain."

It was easier to talk to the boy than to his mom. "Can you take on any shape? A dog? A box? A phoenix?" Mythological creatures had been one of his favorite lessons that winter. Every time the class talked about any of them—dragons, griffons, unicorns, phoenixes—he'd giggle with glee.

Scout shook his head, eyes wide.

Next to her, Thorn patted her leg. "We can take on any humanoid form. We can alter our color and a bit of our girth, but for the most part, we can't overly change our shape."

After she acclimated to the shot of electricity that traversed her body, Viera smiled up at Thorn. "Good to know. So ... what happens now? All I have is ... well, me."

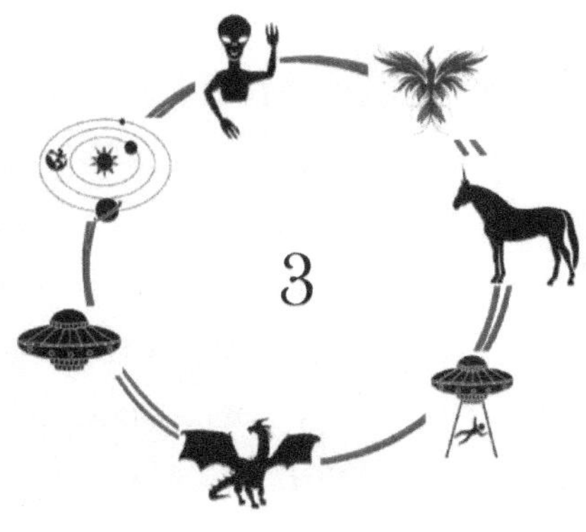

3

Ms. Kor, a Stowaway

Scout

Mom and Ms. Kor disappeared into one of the empty bedrooms, and Scout couldn't believe his teacher, his *human* teacher, had transmitted up to the ship with him. *It's so amazing!* He did a dance.

I can't believe she's here. I hope she loves it. Will it be too much? She handled being on a ship pretty well, but what will happen when she meets Horax? Well, everyone loves Horax. But what about Beaver? I hope she loves Beaver. Beaver is the best.

After a few minutes, Mom stepped into to the hallway with a wary look. "Okay, Scout. We need to discuss this disappearing act you played."

"But, Mom, I had to give Ms. Kor her mug!"

She sighed. "It could've waited. It isn't the end of the school year, it's just spring break."

"But what if you win? We could go home!" Excitement exploded in his body, and he jumped up and down as they walked towards his room.

The ship was small, and it didn't have any family units. His set of rooms was next door to hers.

Thinking about the goal of the trip, he spun, all his excitement turning to energy. *I know Mom will be amazing at the summit. She's done all her homework. She's prepared.*

"Goodness, boy." Mom's voice pulled him from his thoughts. "If you have this much energy, you can run my errands." Mom smiled at Scout's antics, like she always did.

"Sure, Mom. What do you need?" Scout bounced on his toes, waiting for her response.

She gave him a list, then swatted his backside to send him off. He grinned and headed down to the lower levels of the ship. He found Juniper, one of the crew who never left the ship. "Hi, Juni!"

This was Juniper's first time working on a ship. She'd just graduated from school back home. She'd been one of Scout's neighbors and always loved working with different technology. He loved that she worked in engineering. "Hiya, Scout. You made it. I heard you were lost."

He rolled his eyes. "It's not like people on the ship can't pick me up from anywhere on Earth. All this fuss for little old me."

She laughed. "We need to know where you are to beam you up, friend. More like so much hassle from such a tiny person."

He scrunched his face at her. Then giggled. "Okay, maybe." He shrugged.

"So, tell me, why'd you come down here? Just to entertain me?"

"Oh! Yeah. When I was transmitted up, my teacher was caught in the beam. She's on the ship."

"Oh, crap! What are we going to do? There's not time. Is your mom freaking out?"

He snorted. "She never freaks out."

"Fair. So, what's the plan?"

He bit his lip. He didn't want to forget anything. "Mom said we need to make sure she is comfortable while here." He handed her a piece of paper. "These are the measurements she pulled from the computer from the transfer. She wants you to fill her closet with outfits—pants, tops, you know, the full set of stuff. And I'm to get an ear clip for her. I'll show her how to use it tomorrow."

Juniper took the paper and looked it over. "I can do this. We should have all the clothes she needs in our reserves. I can get her moved in and feeling welcome in the next hour or two. But I have a few other projects I need to finish up first."

She ran through a door in the back of the room, then returned with a box. "Here's the ear clip. Do you know how to get it set up?"

"I do. I'll have it ready for her by breakfast." He bounced on his toes, excited to be able to bring his favorite teacher into his world ... finally.

"Sounds good. Tell your mom I'm here if she needs to complain about pesky kids."

Scout laughed as he left her domain.

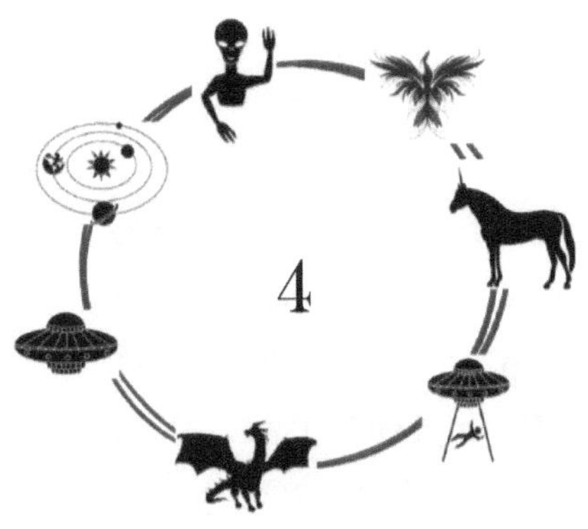

Good Ship Ziner

Viera

Some internal clock had Viera sitting up. She wasn't in her room, which meant the previous evening hadn't been a dream. *Or a nightmare.*

So ... aliens are real, and I'm on a spaceship. Interesting.

She pulled her covers back and trudged out of bed. She never knew one could trudge out of bed, but the previous night Thorn had brought her to this room and let her mind acclimate. Her body felt off. She wasn't sure what it was, but something was

... wrong. *You're on a spaceship, genius. Maybe it's that?*

She took stock of the rooms she'd been assigned. It had a small bedroom with a dresser and closet. There was a receiving room with a couch, small round table with two chairs, and a display Viera didn't know how to use in a language she didn't speak, and a door that led to the restroom.

That last was her current destination. She took a shower. The ship didn't use water. It was a technology Viera didn't understand. She'd been good at math and science when in school. Her teachers said she should teach math at a higher level, but she loved the idea of elementary school. Despite that, she was pretty sure, on this ship, she'd be a luddite in the technological topics.

Clean. *Clean? Am I clean?* She rubbed her arms and they felt soft, like after a good bath back home. She sniffed herself ... *all good.* It all seemed weird and off.

The closet contained a selection of clothes that fit her. Most of it could pass as eccentric Earth-wear. She selected a pair of dark gray linen pants, a green doublet top, and a thick black belt.

Returning to the restroom, she gazed at her reflection. There was a brush, and she managed to arrange her short, straight brown hair in a semblance of a style. *Good thing I have an easy upkeep for school!*

She squinted her eyes to take in the full look. Her blue eyes gazed back. It wasn't horrible. *I could take this outfit to a fair and fit right in!*

A knock on her door brought her out of her thoughts.

Scout stood with a mischievous grin on his face. Gone was his human appearance. He wore a pair of khaki shorts and a yellow shirt with a human eating a burger on it. "Wanna tour of the Ziner?"

All the colors of his outfit hurt Viera's eyes and the word he said didn't make any sense. "Wow, that's a bright shirt! And what did you say? The what?"

"The Ziner, our ship." He held out a hand.

"Oh, yeah. And tell me everything. I feel like a fish out of water."

He laughed. "First of all, Mom said to give you this." He held out something that looked like a combination of an ear bud and an ear clip.

He helped her to clip it on the side of her ear. "What is it?"

Without answering, he leaned towards the ear without the contraption and said ... something. The sound washed through her like a breeze. She shook her head at him, confused. He tittered, then leaned towards the other ear. She heard a bit of a strange noise, but then words became clear. "... me? Can you understand me? Can you—"

"Yes, I can. Oh, my goodness, a translator!" Excitement and wonder bubbled in me. *They have the technology to allow aliens to communicate! Of course, they do ...*

His head bobbed up and down. "There you go. Now I can speak in my normal language, which is easier. There will be other beings you'll run into, and they don't know English. The microphone is very sensitive, so you should be good."

"Wow," she said, "it's like magic!"

The boy snickered and the noise seemed to attract a huge, furry ... beast that barreled from around a corner and stopped in front of Scout, its furry butt wagging in the air. The large moth-looking creature stood maybe two feet tall, a tawny color, with foot long furry wings curled on its back.

A pair of antennae reached towards Scout as its big black eyes stared at him in apparent adoration.

Viera bit back a squawk. "What is that thing?"

"You mean Beaver?"

"That thing is a beaver on your planet?"

Scout held his belly and laughed. "No, silly, it's a ven. Her name is Beaver! She's my pet."

"Oh, yeah, of course. And how did you come up with such a cute name?" Normally, Viera was good with eight-year-olds, but now she felt like she was out of her element.

"Before we got to your planet I'd read a book and there were pictures of beavers. I thought their teeth looked like Beaver's antennae." He beamed.

Viera massaged her temples but could see the connection ... sort of. Maybe. In an eight-year-old's mind. "Wait, you've been at the school since kindergarten. You were reading at five?"

His blush turned his turquoise skin a deep green. "My people age slower than yours. I'm not really eight. Once I finish fourth or fifth grade, we probably will move. On my next birthday, I'll turn twenty-four. I just ... I'm more like the eight-year-olds on your planet in most ways, just a bit more mature."

They'd been walking through corridors with rooms that Viera assumed went to private residences, but at that, she stopped and gaped. *At twenty-four, he's close to my age.* "You're ... twenty-three? Do you get bored in class surrounded by eight-year-olds?"

He reached up and grabbed her hand. "Not really. I mean, I can usually stay home alone, unlike my friends, but for the most part I like kids my age ... I mean kids that look my age. I'm not like people our age. You're close to my age, right?"

Mind spinning fast, she could only nod.

He smiled wide. "Just think of me as eight, it's mostly the right way to think of me." His smile warmed her heart, but it was still confusing.

"Uh-huh. Got it."

At that, he giggled. "It's okay, Ms. Kor, you'll get used to it all."

That or lose my mind, kid.

He showed her the calisthenics area, the entertainment floor, and ended with the mess hall. When they entered, she froze. Sitting at a table across the room were two dragons. They weren't as large as the creatures of myth, but they were dragons—iridescent blue and green scales, tails, wings, and scary.

Viera gaped at them, trying not to ... but ... dragons?

The large beasts didn't even acknowledge their presence as she stared at them, gob-smacked.

Scout tugged on her arm. "Don't worry about the qynad, they're friendly."

"The what now?" She thought her translator had malfunctioned. She tapped at her ear just in case.

"The qynad. What you people would call 'dragons.' They're excellent tacticians. We asked them to help us with the summit. And one of them is a crewmember on the ship. He's one of my best friends."

He dragged her to a table where his mom sat. Someone who looked like Thorn and Scout placed a plate with eggs, bacon, and hash browns in front of her. Viera's stomach let her know its opinions on waiting this long to eat. Then a mug of coffee appeared. Looking up, she saw Thorn had brought it for her. "I'm guessing you need something familiar. The ship can produce most meals, and since we've been on Earth, many of us have gotten used to your traditional offerings, especially coffee."

"Oh, thank goodness. Without coffee, I may have lost it!" Viera teased.

Thorn smiled, and Viera's heart fluttered.

"After breakfast, would you like to join me up at the main deck? I can show you some places on the ship that Scout can't. After that, either Scout can continue to show you around, or if you'd like, you can spend some downtime in your room. We should be arriving at Torville Station Number Six later this afternoon."

It was a lot of information, but Viera nodded, finished her food, and delighted in her coffee. As much as the trip itself had been an unexpected scare, the idea of no coffee was unimaginable.

GPS

Viera

After breakfast, Thorn led the way to what looked to be a regular elevator. Scout followed, because he would lead her back after her visit to the heart of the ship. "Has Scout told you about the lifts?"

"Um ... no?" She smiled down at the boy. "He explained about Beaver, after he ... she ... it? After the pet came bounding down the hall. There was also the explanation of age. Apparently, your son is only a few years younger than me."

"Beaver's a she!" Scout said proudly.

Thorn's deep purple eyebrows rose as she visibly tried not to laugh. "I'm glad my son worked through the important things. Yes, we are a long-lived race. Did he tell you our designation?"

Viera's mouth opened then shut.

With a gentle smile, Thorn turned to face Viera. "As I told you before, we are the chanzii. We are proud but peaceful beings. Our planet was invaded several years ago, and we evacuated to survive. A group of us ended up on your planet because we could blend in."

"Are there other races you can blend in with?"

They reached a door and Thorn typed on the keypad ... or what Viera thought was the keypad. "Yes and no. There are, but some worlds took in chunks of our society without the need. There are a great number of civilizations that have learned interstellar travel. No one planet could take in all of us, so my people had to separate."

A deep sorrow imbued Thorn's voice as she spoke about her people. Sadness built in Viera at the thought of a planet of people ... beings, being forced to evacuate because of another group. "I'm so sorry," she whispered, placing her hand on the other woman's upper arm.

Thorn tilted her head towards the opening doors. "The, ah, lift isn't like an Earth elevator. The paths are omni-directional. It will take you up and down as well as laterally around the ship. The first few rides on the contraption will be a bit of a shock. Let me know if you get dizzy or nauseous."

Viera let her hand drop. Thorn had changed the subject, and she wanted to respect that. They stepped into the lift. It felt like a nice-sized elevator. Again, Thorn typed on a keypad and the doors slid shut. The sound was reminiscent of Star Trek. It made Viera giggle.

Thorn's eyes slid to her. She shook her head. "Scout gave me the translator ... thank you for that, but is there a way to learn the keyboards?"

Scout snickered.

She watched Thorn's beautiful face scrunch as she debated her answer. "Learning a whole new language to understand the keypad for a few days seems a bit excessive. However, there are some school-level lessons you can play with on the computer, but I'm not sure if it's worth it for the few days you're here."

Viera wrinkled her nose as she thought. "I mean, it's something to do, right?"

Thorn shrugged. "Okay, Scout, show Viera a school module once we're done." Her tone made it sound like Viera asked to do a baby's lesson, but Viera didn't care. She liked to learn, and this may be the only way.

"On it, Mom."

The odd feeling from when she woke up came back to visit, along with a few friends. The floor under her feet tilted and her vision darkened as if the lights were going out. She started to sway.

"Whoa, there." Thorn slid an arm around Viera's shoulders. "You okay?"

"Yeah, I think so." All her thoughts were on the tingling in her body from where the arm touched her. "I'm fine."

The doors finally opened, and they entered a large, domed room. Near the front sat three chanzii, one gazing forward at their display, the others at the front screen. In the center were two other workstations. One of the dragon-looking creatures, the qynad, sat at the station to the left, alongside a huge, hairy ... being ... that looked like the legendary Bigfoot. In the back of the room— "back" meaning far from the screen—were two more of the chanzii and the other dragon beast.

The elevator shut, and Viera tried not to gape. She took a few calming breaths, then realized Thorn had said something to her. "What?"

Thorn uttered a soft laugh. "Welcome to the control center of the bridge. This is where the crew normally operates. I wanted you here to see one of the marvels of our time."

To her right, a voice rumbled out: "A marvel of any time. No one's going to be able to recreate it."

Viera opened and shut her mouth a few times. Then Scout bounced. "Hi, Horax!" He waved.

The dragon dipped his head. His blue scales shone in the ship's lights. "Scout. Have you been behaving?"

"I have! How long until GPS?"

Viera shook her head. "You get around using GPS?"

Horax made a gravelly sound which she thought just may be a laugh. "Yes, youngling. We tapped into your planet's communications. When we learned you knew of the GPS, we decided you were worth investigating."

Scout laughed loudly, getting the attention of the rest of the crew. "But, Horax, on Earth it's a global position system, it's how they navigate their cars or ... you know, whatever."

The dragon's tail twitched. "Are you telling me the people of Earth don't know about the Galactic Portal Structure?"

As Scout pronounced, "No!" with amused glee, Viera mouthed, 'portal' with amazed awe.

She turned to Thorn. "You use portals to get to places?"

The other woman smiled warmly. "Yes."

"And the acronym is the same as the one we use on Earth?"

Thorn laughed. "It comes from an elder race. The fact that the letters matched is still being studied by some scholars."

Viera's eyes widened. "Really?"

Horax scoffed. "No." He rotated to face her ready to lecture, like a seasoned professor. "The portals have been in place for hundreds of your Earth years, maybe even more. There aren't many portal points, but from them, you can dart to any of the others, as long as you know the key to getting around. They aren't secret. Part of how they were constructed protects from collisions within or directly at the entrance and exit of the structures.

It's fantastic and complicated. Way above my pay-grade."

Viera stepped towards the dragon, her fear turning to a thirst to learn. "Who created them? What is the mechanism for their construction?"

Thorn's warm hand landed gently on her shoulder. "You are welcome to ask all of these questions, but not right now. We're still in a hurry. If you get Horax talking, we'll never get him to stop. Once we reach Torville Station Number Six, you're welcome to sit with the qynad and discuss the minutiae of GPS to your heart's content."

Some People's Children

Betsy

Betsy sat at her desk, sorting through all the papers. She had too many clients. *When did this happen? Why did this happen? With all these responsibilities, I don't have time to study.*

She gazed at her bookcase and sighed. *I wish Dad were around. He'd be able to help me with some of this. Even grandpa Gan-dolt. As much of a pain in the ass as he was, he was good with all of that.*

With a final shake of her head, she returned to her paperwork. It was Saturday afternoon, and she didn't want to spend any more time in the office on the weekend than necessary. Weekends should be for relaxing. *Yeah, right!*

Betsy checked her watch. Her phone should be charged. Dragging herself up from her chair, she headed over to a panel on the wall and pulled out the phone. *Three missed texts from Viera's mom? Huh?*

There was a lot of work she needed to get done, but the kooky old lady never contacted her. She'd only gotten her number from Viera because her friend didn't have many close friends in the area and her mother was way over-protective.

The first text had come in at ten that morning. Betsy thought about it and realized she'd been ignoring her texts all day to catch up on paperwork. As she listened to her music, her phone's battery had dipped low enough that she wanted to charge it. She shook her head and perused the texts.

Ms. Doeth, you may not know me, but I'm Viera Kor's mother. She gave me your number and told me that if I ever needed to reach out to you I could, and you'd be okay with it. I just wanted to see if you'd heard from my daughter. I set her up on a perfectly respectable date last night and

Donald said she never showed up. He never got a text or call either. Please let me know if you hear from her. Thank you. Ms. Kor - Viera's mother.

Betsy rubbed her temples. She wasn't sure if she should laugh or roll her eyes at the length or formality of the text. Had no one taught this woman what proper quick texting was? If she wanted to add that much detail, then why not call?

With a sigh, she read the next text, time stamped eleven-thirty. *Did you get my text? I can never tell. Please text me back. Viera isn't answering her texts or phone calls. I hope she's okay.*

The last text read much the same.

Betsy looked over her desk and sighed. She navigated to Viera's number. The call went to voicemail. "Hey, Viera. I'm not sure what happened last night, but good for you for avoiding another forced blind date. Do me a favor, call your mom. I'll do the same. I'm sure you're just relaxing, watching movies, and your phone died ... again. You really need to get better with technology." She realized how hypocritical that last bit was and snorted. "You don't have to call, just ... I'll see you Tuesday."

She put down her phone and shook her head. *Viera, what game are you playing with your mother? I know she annoys you, but this is silly.* Then again, Betsy had lost both her parents years ago. What did she have to say in the matter?

Gazing down at the paperwork, she decided she was done. It was time to head out and be young for the rest of the weekend. *Well, as young as I can be at my age!*

7

One Big Family

Viera

The ship docked with a jerk and Viera flew from her bed landing hard on the floor. She rolled across the room, slamming into the wall. She'd been dreaming about being on a ship ... *but I am on a ship ... about to board a space station. What has happened to my life?*

A soft knock echoed through Viera's room. The sound startled her from her musings. She realized she was in a weird position against the wall, arm angled over her head. She wiggled to get into a better, more comfortable angle. The learning tablet sat next to her with the last lesson she'd worked through.

It had taken Scout a few minutes and a call to Horax to figure out how to switch the learning English lesson into learning chanziian. Viera now knew why Thorn had seemed so dubious about her learning the language. This would not be a simple exercise. She only needed it for the week. It was kind of silly to work so hard when she wouldn't use it once she returned to Earth.

With a grunt, Viera got to her feet and opened the door. Scout smiled up at her. "We're here, we're at Torville Station Number Six! Come on!" His exuberance was infectious. Above him flew Beaver.

He all but dragged Viera through the corridors until they met up with his mom. Viera smiled shyly. "Hi, Thorn ... er, Ms. Firoza, um, do you have a title I should use when we're around other chanzii?"

Thorn laughed. "Thorn is still fine. When we're on the station, my people will call me Commander Firoza, but I'm not your commander, so it wouldn't make sense. Thorn works for me."

Scout smiled up at his mom. "Mom's the youngest Commander our world has trusted in ages. She's really good at what she does."

Viera's eyebrows rose. "Is that so? And how young are you?"

The other woman's smile grew. "On Earth, that's a rather rude question, Ms. Kor. On my planet, age is worn as a badge. As it goes, our planet's cycle both in daily rotation and its yearly path, is very close to Earth's. We have closer to twenty-eight of your standard hours a day, but our yearly travel is three-hundred-thirteen days."

Scout spun in place. "Mom made me do the math when we landed. You have eight-thousand seven-hundred-sixty hours in a year. Our planet has eight-thousand seven-hundred sixty-four. That's almost the same. Cool, right?"

Viera couldn't help it; she laughed. "It certainly is, kiddo. Look at all the math you've done."

His eyes widened, then he smiled.

As they slowly made their way from the Ziner to Torville Station Number Six, Viera noticed everyone held a bag. She sighed. "What should I do about clothes and other things?"

Thorn nodded. "We requested a suite of rooms, bigger than we normally have. You'll be able to stay with us, if that's okay with you. I also ordered up a few outfits for you. I don't know your exact size, but they should work. The things I ordered aren't form-fitting."

Viera blushed. The idea of Thorn dressing her made her uncertain feeling for the woman morph into something more intimate. "Oh, um, thanks. That sounds ... good."

"I have credit at most of the shops. If you need anything, just give them my name. Don't worry about the cost. I can cover it."

Her cheeks heated more. "Oh ... I can pay you back. You don't have to buy me things."

Thorn rubbed her arm. "First of all, I know how little Earth teachers are paid. Second, it's my son's fault you're here. Third, it's really no problem. Nothing in the station is that expensive. I can cover it."

Viera was about to say more when they were suddenly *on* the station. The corridor was large, really large. It looked big enough to hold half the animals at a circus, side by side, then stacked atop each other.

She shivered at the cool temperature, and the number of people ... beings ... *aliens!* ... moving around was astounding. Her brain couldn't even begin to catalog what it saw.

"Come on, Ms. Kor, this way! Let's go!"

They squeezed through fur and scales, Beaver flying above them. The moth carried two bags strapped to her back. As they scurried to find their rooms, Viera thought she saw other beasts of legend, but her mind was on maximum overload, and following Thorn and Scout was about all she could manage.

It took two turns before they were in a corridor without throngs of other beings. Thorn breathed out audibly. "This summit is going to be a nightmare. Viera, Scout, I suggest we eat in our suite tonight and get some rest ... tomorrow the games begin."

Definitely Not Kansas

Viera

Viera sat at the small dining table in the family suite Thorn and Scout had been assigned. She'd woken up early and decided to practice more of their language. As she sat, struggling with the alphabet, she grumbled, "All I want is a coffee with a bit of sugar and milk, is that so much to ask for?"

Her head pounded as the swirls and dots that made up the chanzii alphabet stared back at her.

A metallic voice next to her intoned. "One sweetened tall coffee with milk." Behind her there was a whirring sound. As the tantalizing aroma of coffee surrounded her, she turned to see a mug sitting in a slot in the wall, steam rising over the rim.

"I don't know who you are, metallic voice, but thank you." She carefully took the warm mug, brought it to her nose and sniffed. Instantly, she relaxed. It was a bit too hot to drink, so she finished her lesson and then started sipping the luxurious brew.

It didn't take long for Thorn to walk in from the hallway. "Morning, fire cloud."

Viera opened her mouth, then shut it. Her eyes narrowed as she thought about what Thorn said. "Fire cloud?"

At a wall, Thorn typed on a panel. "Oh, sorry." She yawned. "Can you grab my coffee? I'll order us up some breakfast."

Viera turned to find another steaming mug.

Thorn was back at the digital input device. "On our planet, 'fire cloud' is a term of endearment, something well appropriate in this situation. What is it you say on Earth?"

After another sip of coffee, Viera said, "Morning, sunshine?"

Beaver ran in and Viera dropped her hand to pet the moth-like ... Viera thought hard ... *ven! That's it. Beaver is a ven!*

She heard the whirring sound again and a bowl of food appeared in the wall slot. Bringing it to the table, she stared at it dubiously. "This looks ... interesting."

Thorn laughed. "It's for Beaver. I'll start on ours next. I heard the crazy ven running around from my room and it's impossible to eat if she's not fed. Put the bowl on the floor?"

Viera did and the creature swooped in to eat.

At the next sound, Viera found something that looked like a warm cereal. There were two bowls. The grain was covered with fruit Viera didn't recognize and nuts. "Should I be concerned about if I can eat all of this?"

Sitting across from her, Thorn slid one of the bowls to herself. "No, there's nothing to worry about. We use the same replication technology back on Earth. The representatives that know we're there have tried the foods I'm feeding you. If you can eat fruits and nuts, you can have this."

With a happy nod, Viera dug in. It tasted better than it looked. The fruit was sweet and juicy, like a cross between a cherry and an apple, and the nuts added an Earthy saltiness. The grain was similar enough to the hot cereals she'd eaten back home, and not very interesting.

Once her belly wasn't grousing at her, she looked up at Thorn. "So, your summit starts today. You'll be busy from sun-up to sundown ... or, you know, whatever it is you use for time around here."

"We use the galactic standard. It's a thirty-hour clock. The day starts at G-nine. There is a break for a midday meal at G-fifteen. The final meal of the day tends to be at G-twenty-two. The sleeping block goes from G-twenty-eight until G-seven, for most adults. Kids go to bed earlier, and often wake up earlier."

Viera gazed down at her fitness watch. Sunday, five a.m. "I don't know that my watch will help with all of this. With the three-day summit, how does that fit with us getting back in time?"

"We have time. The days are only a bit longer, and we have the weekend on the other end as well."

"Okay, that's true. So, am I stuck in here the whole time?" She knew she could continue her lessons, but intensive alien language study wasn't the exact staycation she'd planned.

Scout ran in and slammed into his mom. "Can I take Veira to the game level and then get lunch?" Before Thorn could answer, he darted to the panel and started pounding away. He zipped to grab a bowl of something less healthy-looking than what she had before Veira could grab it for him.

Thorn looked in his bowl and pursed her lips. "That sounds good—" Scout squealed. "—but sweetie, remember, she is new to all this. You'll have to take things slow. Introduce her to all the things she doesn't know."

Veira wasn't sure she liked the sound of that.

Thorn gave her a sympathetic smile. "Later this evening, maybe you and I can get dinner together." Viera's heart pounded hard in her chest. Was Thorn asking her out on a date? "I'd like to check in with you without the small one pestering us." *She's probably just feeling responsible for me since I'm here because of Scout.*

Trying not to slump at her misunderstanding, Viera nodded. "Sounds great."

The lift closed behind them and all Viera could see were the wine and black scales of the largest dragon ... qynad ... she'd ever seen. Since it was the third one she'd seen, her sample size wasn't large. She wanted to yelp, but Scout seemed calm, so she tried to play it cool.

He gazed up at her. "You okay, Ms. Kor? That's just Voran. He's nice!"

Nice, right. Could eat me in a single bite, but we'll go with 'nice.' She nodded down at the boy, then gaped as the qynad moved away and a room full of creatures walking and flying all around them was revealed. Trying not to tremble, she dragged Scout to a small table and sat, Beaver hot on their heels.

"Okay, so dragons are qynads. That um—" She swallowed, not wanting to say the first thing that came to mind. "Bird of paradise?"

Scout looked up and searched until he found the red and orange bird with feathers dripping down its body in what looked like fire. "Oh! That's a tindrex! They're elusive. Only here because of the summit. Like Mom, the clan must've brought extras since that one isn't busy."

Viera realized her breathing was rough but didn't care. This was a lot. "So, it isn't the mythical phoenix that ultimately burns up from its death, reemerging anew from its ashes?"

They both watched as the creature flew and swooped, eventually landing on a branch of a tree that grew along the edge of the large room. The leaves of the tree were large and had a blue tint. The bark was a greenish brown. There were yellow highlights all up and down the plant and something on it, alive or added by the station personnel, glowed. "No, not a phoenix. That's a made-up Earth word, like dragon, but it does live forever ... like you said."

She froze. "You're kidding, right? Teasing me?"

"Why would I tease you? Mom said to make sure you understood." His face was so open.

A unicorn walked across the promenade, approached a Bigfoot looking creature. They spoke a few words, then it returned the way they'd come. Viera's eyes were wide as she clicked her mouth shut. "Unicorns? They're real?" Her every dream from childhood was coming true. She imagined riding on the unicorn across a field, flowers cascading behind them in a rainbow of petals.

"Unicorn?" Scout's voice brought her back to the space station. "Oh, no! That's a yonat; they're the Elders."

In a soft voice to herself, she whispered. "Ah, so no riding them across a field of flowers."

"Riding?" He sounded scandalized, which was impressive for one so young ... or not so young. "No, no one would ever think to ride a yonat. They're the ones Mom's approaching with her request for help."

Viera watched where the beautiful white creature had disappeared. "Oh ... got it. The yonat are the Elders. What is the person they came out to speak with?" She waved in case Scout missed it.

Beaver, bored with their talk, flew off to join the tindrex on the tree branch. Scout watched his pet fly off with a happy expression. "Oh, Tim? He's a fing."

Viera's eyebrows rose. "The Bigfoot looking creature is a fing, and his name is Tim?"

Scout nodded. "Yep, you're getting there."

"No wonder you always looked so amused in class. We learned about all these fantasy creatures, but to you, they were all real. Not only that, the names we had for them were wrong. You were probably sitting there thinking about friends while I discussed them as if they were all imaginary."

Scout rocked in his seat. "It's not that bad, Ms. Kor. I knew that the people around me were blind."

She rubbed her arms. The weird feelings were getting worse. She felt nauseous. *Maybe I'm allergic to the food Thorn ordered up for me this morning. Just because other Earthlings ... heh, Earthlings—* she tried to hide her snort—*can eat those ingredients, doesn't mean I can.*

She swallowed as her body swayed in her seat. She didn't want Scout to know she wasn't feeling well so she turned to gaze at all the other beings walking around. The woozy feelings made her insensible to the fantastical sights around her.

She kept smiling as Scout pointed out more and more around her.

"Scout," a grumbly voice brought Viera back to the present. "Have you told our friend here about the magic bath?"

The boy's green eyes widened. "No, Horax, it didn't occur to me. But it should've, shouldn't it? She doesn't know about magic, does she?"

The smaller blue dragon sighed. His body took up the space of a mini car, so thinking of him as small was ironic. His tail twitched as he faced her. "Young Viera. Your planet is saturated in magic. Being one of the few creatures that doesn't use magic, your planet is a well of power. You need to soak in the element; your body is probably craving it."

Viera shook her head, convinced she was losing her mind. "Magic? Are you teasing me?"

"No. How do you think the chanzii shift shape? What do you think powers the GPS?"

"The GPS? Isn't that technology?"

"It's imbued technology, master craftsmanship that utilizes magic. It's almost a living item. We can discuss it more later. You need to go soak. Three rounds, I believe, by your tremors. Then you'll need to eat and rest. Becoming depleted isn't good for you ... for anyone really. While off-planet we all soak every morning. Coming from a magic-rich planet, you should do a double each morning, or soak morning and night."

Her head swam with the information. She barely noticed as Scout took her hand and led her away. First there were aliens, then portals, and now magic. What was next—one ring to bind them all?

9

The Summit

Thorn

This was it. All Thorn's studying and planning since she'd landed on Earth had been to prepare for these three days. Two days, really. Two days for her to present her case with Major Shifts, and on the third day the Elders would come to their final decision.

Major Shifts was dressed much as she was, except his bands depicted his rank. His hair hung to his shoulders in soft waves. The compassion that normally shone from his jewel-green eyes was hardened by what needed to be done at these proceedings.

Thorn gazed at the three representatives of the krottel and held back a sneer. They all stood in their capes, the hoods overlapping their masks. *Why do they always cover up from head to foot? Gloves, masks, the works? What do they have to hide? Or are they that insecure in the strangeness?* She shivered. *I can't imagine what argument those assholes can bring to these proceedings. Fucking planet-killers. Go kill an elder planet, see what happens then, fucken jerks!*

She stood at the table assigned to the chanzii, her eyes fixed on the Elder Flower Prancer. He was her best hope, being as young as he was. Elder Star Dancer was much older and a stickler for rules. She believed in the rights of all creatures to live their evolutionary lives as they would unfold. This council was created to enforce one rule, the concept of noninterference, the first rule of the galactic council. It was rumored she wrote and refined the fine print and the wording on their manifesto.

Flower Prancer, the spokesbeing of the summit, stepped to the center of the three tables. "Friends, beings from across the galaxy, and in some cases, foes. We welcome you to the chamber. I will remind you that this is a silent chamber. Nothing that happens during the summit will be discussed beyond this arena. If I, or any of my brethren, learn that the silence has been broken, punishment will be swift."

Despite the severity of the words, there wasn't much reaction from the assembled creatures. Everyone there knew the rules. The summit, as with all council meetings, was private. Pieces of the debates could be discussed, but those topics would be made clear at the end of the proceeding.

"Commander Firoza, if you'll start."

One of the krottel glided forward.

What is it with those beings? How do they always move so smoothly and silently? They're creepy. They were creepy when they invaded our planet, and they are awful now.

"I must object, Elder Flower Prancer. Why does the chanzii speak first?" Its voice was cold and monotonous.

A cold wave went through the arena. Flower Prancer stared flatly at the krottel until the being glided back to its table. Then Flower Prancer repeated, "Commander Firoza."

Thorn's mouth went dry, and her body began to tremble. There were so many creatures in the room, and all their attention shifted to her. After a shaky breath, she licked her lips and gave a curt nod. "Thank you, Elder. My people are not violent. As a whole, we get along amongst ourselves and the beings of other worlds. We were surprised when the krottel sent warships to Abritos, our planet, and demanded our immediate evacuation."

She slowly spun, taking in the faces of the people in the crowd. "We as a people had no idea why we were being told to leave our homes, our countries, our planet." She shook her head, the memory bringing a renewed sadness. Major Shifts came up next to her and placed a supporting hand on her shoulder. She nodded in thanks. "We didn't show our bellies in fear; we fought, but when we realized we would lose and not only lose soldiers, but kids, the elderly, the innocent, we as a people made a hard decision ... we left our planet to save ourselves."

Murmurs went up around the room. Rubbing her face, Thorn realized tears flowed freely down her cheeks.

"I am here to ask the Elders to put sanctions on the krottel. In my research, I have found that Abritos is not the first, but the fifth planet they've taken. Each planet ends up dead in under twenty-five years. All life: plants, animals, beings, are dead and gone, and the krottel move on to the next. This has got to stop. Or they are going to systematically annihilate our galaxy."

10

We All Need To Eat

Viera

"If you press this yellow button in the shower, you get soaked in magic. A blue light turns on when the soak starts and turns off when it's done. That's it." Scout's eyes were wide as he explained as if he wanted to run from the bathing room as fast as he could. "Good?"

"I think I'm good. Once I'm done, I'll need your help with ordering up a meal. Can I get something Earth-based? Maybe pasta or chicken soup?"

Scout shuffled his feet. "Could we have pizza? Mom doesn't love pizza, so we rarely have it."

Viera huffed out a laugh. "Pizza sounds perfect."

He skipped out of the room, shutting the door behind himself. She sighed and followed him out into her room in time to hear the main door of her room shut. She opened her closet and selected navy-blue linen pants and a sage green doublet. There was no reason to select a different belt. From what she could tell, one belt was the same as all the others.

Back in the bathing room, she stepped into the shower and started with cleaning off. After a couple of days with the alien version of washing, she decided she liked it. Once that part was done, she hit the yellow button. The blue light turned on, and her body started to tingle. Viera placed her hands on the wall as a tremble passed down her body.

The cycle took a few minutes. Taking the advice given to her seriously, she tapped the button again and then a third time. After the light went out, she took a deep breath and realized she felt better, more centered, than she'd felt since the aliens had beamed her up.

Clean, dressed, and full of magic—*magic! Holy shit!*—she headed out to meet Scout for lunch.

On the table was a pizza with sausage and black olives. "We can watch a movie. Do you want to watch a movie? Horax said to relax, and a movie is relaxing." His words tumbled out of his mouth.

"Is there a movie you want to watch?"

His face morphed into a mischievous smile with his sparkling eyes. She didn't trust it at all. "How about *Lord of The Rings*?" he asked, face open and hopeful.

"How about 'no,' bud-o? You are not old enough for that movie."

"I'm over twenty," he whined.

"You are a student in my second-grade class. I just can't say yes to that. How about *Never-Ending Story*? I love that movie."

His head tilted. "I don't know that one." He typed something on a panel. "Oh! It has a shasul in it, coolio!" A few more clicks and a wall shimmered, and the movie started.

Viera sat and served two plates up with pizza. Scout dropped into a chair next to her with an, "Oof" and dug into his food.

They spent the next hour and a half eating and watching the movie. The normalcy of the activity centered Viera. She enjoyed the movie as well as Scout's reaction to the film.

"There is no such thing as that creature!" he scoffed.

"They got the ears wrong!" he said, waving his hand around.

"Naming her wouldn't do that!" he said, face scrunched up in frustration.

In the end, Viera snickered at his investment in something people made up so many years ago on a planet far, far away.

After the movie, Viera rested. She lay on the couch and asked Scout to start *Willow*. Once that movie ended, she requested *The Princess Bride*.

Thorn returned while the last movie played. She squinted. "Horax told me Scout forgot to mention magic to you. Are you feeling better?"

Viera rubbed her face with her hands as she sat up. *Magic ... for fuck's sake, everyone just speaks about it like it's your average, everyday thing. Pass me a soda, and have you filled up on your magic?*

"Yeah, I think I'm better. I mean, internally, yeah. Mentally, it's still a lot."

The beautiful smile appeared, and Viera was glad she was sitting. "That's one of the reasons I wanted to have dinner tonight. Let me change, and we can head out to the promenade. There are a few shops."

Though Viera knew the dress-uniform Thorn wore was probably not comfortable, Viera loved the way the pants hugged her ... assets. With a sigh, she gazed down at *her* pants and doublet. "Is what I'm wearing okay?"

Thorn's gaze traveled down and then back up her body. *Did she go slower than was strictly necessary? Was she checking me out?* Viera mentally slapped herself at her own idiocy as the other woman spoke. "I think what you're wearing looks great. I'll just be a sec."

As Thorn sauntered away, Viera realized her heart pounded faster than normal. *Get it together, Viera. This is just a concerned alien checking on the silly stowaway. Nothing more.*

When Thorn walked out, she wore a form-fitting royal blue tank dress that ended mid-thigh. There were cutouts at her waist on each side. Her dark purple hair fell in waves past her shoulders. She held out her hands to Viera to pull her up from the couch. "Ready?"

She licked her suddenly dry lips. "Yeah ... ready."

Earlier, when she and Scout had made it down to the promenade, they'd barely stepped off the lift before Viera had dragged them to a small table. Then Horax had sent them back to their rooms. This time, Thorn led her across the center of the large arena, practically a city block in width with shops and creatures galore, to a shop surrounded by small tables.

One of the Bigfoot beasts, a fing, greeted them. "Thorn! You made it. We have your table ready, just like you requested. We've been busy. I'm glad you made it."

"Bob!" She walked up to him, and they bumped forearms. "Thank you, my good friend."

They headed into the shop and found a table. There were menus, but when Viera picked it up, she couldn't read it. With a sigh, she put it back down.

Thorn placed a hand on Viera's arm—heat tingled through her body at the contact—and said, "I'll help you order."

"This doesn't look like what I've been studying." She rubbed her forehead.

"Oh, you've been learning chanziian. This is written in galactic standard." Thorn's thumb rubbed, distracting Viera from her ire.

"How many languages do you know?"

Thorn's face scrunched up. "Five fluently. A smattering of a few others."

Viera let out a huff of a laugh. "Wow! I barely know English."

"Okay, do you like steak? A form of potatoes? A vegetable? Dessert? Do you trust me?"

Stomach grumbling, Viera nodded. "I do. You know the food here, I don't."

After ordering, Viera observed other groups as they came in to dine. A party of griffins walked by and Viera sighed. Thorn followed her gaze. "What's wrong?"

"I'm just curious what they're called. So much of what I know is just wrong."

"What, the griffins?"

Her head was going to explode. "You're playing with me, aren't you?"

Thorn smiled and Viera blushed. "I'm not, they really are griffins. It's one of the only ones your planet has right."

Viera snorted and shook her head. "Okay, fine. One for the Earthlings."

Thorn slid both of Viera's hands into hers. "I wanted to ask you a question."

She swallowed past the nervous lump suddenly in her throat. "Yeah."

"I feel like there is a tension between us ... you know, a good tension." Thorn's thumbs rubbed the back of Viera's hands, sending chills throughout her body. "And I have to admit, you are lovely." Viera bit back any reaction or sound that tried to escape her. "But you have to understand the difference in our races."

"Are we not compatible?" The words were blurted out before she could stop them.

Thorn chuckled, sending heat to Viera's gut. "No, we are very much compatible. But, despite us being equivalent in the percentage of our lives lived, your lifespan is an eyeblink in comparison to mine, and I want to protect my heart. I would love to spend our time here exploring each other," Thorn broke the eye contact they'd been holding, shutting her eyes and taking a breath. "But when we return to Earth, I think we should go back to the separation we had."

Excitement and disappointment warred in Viera. "Are you saying you want a stress relieving bed mate while I'm here and that's it?"

Thorn bit her lip, a blush coloring her cheeks. "Sorry if that sounds bad." She started to pull her hands away, but Viera held tight.

"I'm not saying 'no,' just clarifying. No pairing that begins with dating assumes a lifelong commitment. Why not play? We're just starting off knowing it's for a bit of fun." She tried to make it sound light, though part of her felt disappointed. *Why? Once this summit is done, won't Thorn and her people leave Earth? Gah! Get your head on straight, Viera!*

Leaning over, Thorn pulled Viera in for a kiss. When their tongues met, Viera deepened the kiss with a groan as the heat in her gut exploded to encompass her whole body. After the kiss ended, Viera wondered at the brazen public display of affection, but since she didn't know any of the aliens around, she just gave Thorn a small smile of appreciation.

With a chuckle, Viera said, "If the kiss is any indication, the next few nights won't be boring at all."

Taking Off The Edge

Viera

Thorn's room was only slightly larger than Viera's. When the door shut, Thorn pushed Viera's back against the wall, and dipped down to continue their kiss.

Viera reached up, sliding her fingers into Thorn's cool long hair, pushing her body against the other woman's well-muscled, yet pliant form.

Her tongue explored, tasting the sweet dessert they'd shared as desire pulsed down to her core. Thorn's hands slowly explored down her sides as Viera's fingers played in her silky strands.

A loosening of the pressure at her waist and a thunk on the ground let her know her belt had been removed.

Thorn kissed over to Viera's ear, nibbling the lobe, then licked her neck. "Mmm. You're tasty. Let's move to the bed and remove our clothes." She backed up and pulled off Viera's top, adding action to words.

The sage top pooled on the floor. Viera unbuttoned the pants, and they slid down her legs. She walked out of them and her shoes. She quickly removed her bra as she watched Thorn unzip and let her dress fall from her utterly perfect body.

There was nothing underneath the dress.

She spent a moment gaping at the other woman before she took a breath, building her resolve, and approached her. When their bodies were barely touching each other, Viera let her hands skim over Thorn's form starting at her thighs and moving up.

Her skin was warm and soft. Reaching around, Viera spent a moment enjoying the taut ass she'd spent more time then she'd be willing to admit admiring. It was every bit as squeezable as she'd imagined.

Thorn made a sound of approval as she kissed and licked up Viera's neck. Her hands rubbed down Viera's shoulders and arms.

Viera slid her hands around Thorn's well-toned abdomen and up her sides until her thumbs found the swell of the other woman's breasts.

While they investigated each other, Thorn had moved them closer to the bed. Viera felt the mattress edge bump into her claves. With a final nibble to her ear, Thorn gave a push, and Viera landed on her back.

Viera scooted until she was fully on the bed. With fire in her eyes, the turquoise goddess crawled up her body, then pushed up on her arms and stared down at her. "I've been wanting to taste you since my son entered your class, Ms. Kor. Tonight, you're my second dessert. We can mix it up tomorrow." Then she dipped her head and ran her slick tongue around one of Viera's breasts slowly until she reached the nipple, sucking it in.

She mirrored the motion with her thumb on Viera's other breast. Then she scraped her teeth on the sensitive skin, pinching lightly, until Viera arched up with a gasp.

"That's it, my sweet Earthling. My lovely fire cloud, I want to hear you."

She left her hand to play as she dragged her mouth down Viera's belly. Viera's sex throbbed with need and want as that skillful mouth got closer and closer. She ached for it.

Just when Viera thought she would burst, Thorn reached her core and licked up her center. Moaning, Thorn focused on her clit, flicking her tongue and sucking.

With skill Viera couldn't fathom, Thorn's fingers slid inside her, probing as her mouth continued to tease and play.

The pleasure built to high electricity as her body trembled. Her breathing got ragged, and her head fell back as her world shrank to Thorn and her mouth and hands, and *Oh, my god!*

Thorn did something with her tongue and finger and Viera screamed, her body fracturing under the other woman's ministrations.

They didn't stop.

The tongue play continued.

The fingers plunged in and out, demanding more.

Viera's body was an instrument at Thorn's mercy and before she knew it a second wave struck and she panted out Thorn's name in joy, in reverence, in shock.

That had never happened to her before.

Her nights would definitely not be boring.

12

Straight From a Horse's Mouth

Viera

Viera woke up wrapped up in Thorn's arms. Something in her settled with how right it felt ... how well they fit together. A piece of her wanted this feeling every morning, a forever peace in her soul.

A low hum rumbled through the other woman as she tensed, then released Viera to stretch. "Morning, fire cloud."

"Morning, sunshine."

Thorn kissed her forehead. "Why don't you slip on your tunic? It'll cover your tantalizingly lovely assets. You can shower and change in your room. See you in the main room in twenty?"

A cold shiver ran down Viera's spine. "Oh, yeah. See you then. You need to get to the summit." She threw on the top and grabbed her pants, bra, shoes, and belt. The dash to her room was quick and she luckily didn't run into Scout or Beaver.

In her room, she selected a wine-colored doublet and black linen pants. She briefly wondered if the colors meant anything. She decided she could ask Scout after Thorn left. In the shower she cleaned off, then soaked in magic ... twice.

She wanted to be sure she was fully prepared for the day. The odd feelings she'd had since arriving had disappeared after she'd soaked the day before, and she didn't want the feeling to return.

Clean, full of magic—*magic! gah!!*—she went out to the main room where Thorn waited. She wore a steel-colored pair of slacks and a matching button-down suit jacket. At the bottom of the jacket, around the collar, and at the wrists, there were light blue bands of color. It was the same, or a similar outfit from the day before.

"We're early," Thorn said, handing her a mug of coffee. "Why don't we head to the promenade for breakfast? Scout can manage himself until you get back."

"Are you sure? Will you be late?" Viera hated how worried she was. Should she be worried about someone who said no strings attached, a virtual stranger? *Do not get attached, Viera!*

"It's not even seven. I have time before the summit begins today. Let's go."

They didn't go to Bob the Bigfoot ... er, fing's establishment for breakfast. Instead, they headed to a place that looked suspiciously like a café. After they sat and Thorn ordered for them, Viera couldn't help herself. "What's this place called? Jitters? The Mocha Stop? Cool Beans?"

"It's called Nebula Hunger Stomper. It sounds better in its native language. Coffee is relatively new to the galaxy. It's Earth's greatest contribution. That and tacos."

Viera snorted. "You're kidding me. Tacos?"

"Well, yes and no, I mean, who doesn't love a good taco? They're becoming a huge hit. Restaurants all over have 'Taco Tuesday' specials, not realizing Tuesday is a day of the week and not part of the special."

The laughing was getting out of control. The type that just looking at your partner in crime made it worse. When their food came, Viera covered her mouth to try to contain her mirth, but it wasn't helping much.

"What seems to be so amusing?" A warm, deep, voice washed over her. Jerking her head to the left, Viera came face to ... snout? with a unicorn. *No, wait; not a unicorn. They're one of the Elders. What are they called? Damn it, think. So many new names! It's damn near impossible to remember them all.*

The beautiful light-gray creature with violet eyes and a rainbow mane and tail gazed at her. Its pointy horn shimmered in the dome's light. "My name is Flower Prancer. I am one of the Yonat." *Yonat! That was it. Remember, Viera, yonat.* She was about to chant the word in her head, but knew she had to focus on the Elder's words. It continued, "And you are?"

She had a feeling he knew ... everyone knew. The idiot human who had somehow ended up on a space station halfway across the galaxy from her home! "Um, hi, Flower Prancer." Her mind reeled at the name. A childhood fantasy of riding a unicorn through a field of flowers, petals in all colors floating behind them, played through her head. She had to suppress a laugh.

An Elder with such a simple name. *Am I being punked?* "My name is Viera. Um, Viera Kor. You can call me Viera." She held out her hand, gaped at it, then dropped it to the table.

Flower Prancer whinnied, and she was pretty sure it was its laugh. "Oh, you are a delight, child." The beautiful beast faced Thorn. "Representative, can you explain to Viera a bit about my species?"

Thorn smiled. "As you know, we've come to the summit because our planet was invaded."

Viera bit her lip. She didn't want to interrupt, but she figured now was as good a time as any to ask questions. "Who invaded? I'm guessing it wasn't the yonat."

Thorn nearly choked and a quiver ran through the unicorn's body. "No, of course not. The Elders would never." Thorn did a final shake of her head. "It was the krottel. I don't know if you've met them. They're a reclusive race when they aren't finding new planets to take over. Ours is the fifth, but only the third that was previously inhabited."

They all got quiet as plates of something that resembled quiche was placed in front of her and Thorn. "Would you like your coffee filled? A dish of food for you, Elder?"

After a quick confirmation nod from Flower Prancer, Thorn smiled up at the server. "Yes, to all of that, thank you."

Viera watched the server leave, took a bite of her food, internally moaned at how good it tasted, then contemplated her table companions. "If these people are invading, why isn't anything being done to stop them?"

Thorn's mouth tightened for a moment. "We tried. My people attempted to defend the planet, but there were so many of the krottel. They swarmed in. I don't know what it is about them, but they're impossible to stop. It became clear that if we wanted to survive as a people, we had to leave our homes, our land, our planet."

"Couldn't you negotiate to coexist?"

Thorn's voice hardened. "No. The krottel made that perfectly clear."

Flower Prancer fidgeted, pawing the ground with their front hoof. "We are working to get to the bottom of the allegations. For now, all we know is the chanzii are all off-world and the krottel have moved in. We don't take galactic sanctions lightly—"

"Or move fast," Thorn mumbled.

"No, child. We don't move quickly. We don't want to make a mistake. The krottel claim that you'd moved from your planet when they arrived. We will work through all the facts—" their tail swished, —from you and the other planets that claim to have been invaded. And if wrongdoing is evident, we, as the Elders, will act. You have my word."

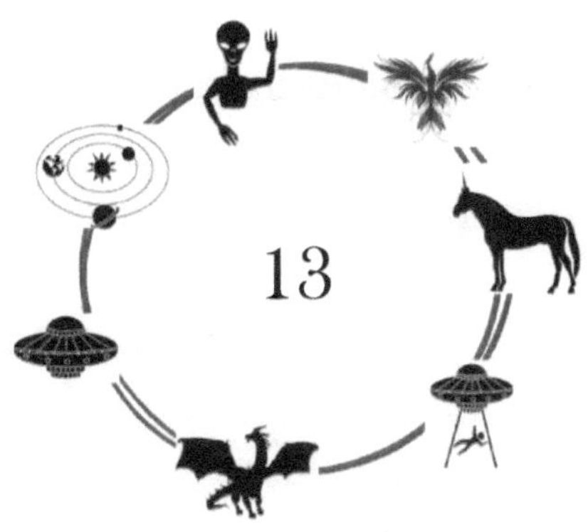

13

The Scallywag

Viera

"Okay," Viera said, finishing off her food. "But why? What are the krottel after? Why do they hop from planet to planet, invading? Do they really need more than one?"

Flower Prancer bobbed their large head. Viera wasn't sure if the yonat was cataloging her questions or approving of them.

They'd finished the warm breakfast cereal in a few bites and continued to talk with the group while they finished theirs. "Those are excellent questions. After Commander Firoza levied her allegations against the krottel, including all five planets they presumably took over, my people went back and did some research of our own. Do you know what we found?"

Viera loved history. Earth was unfortunately built on years of war. "Desolation? Destruction? Destroyed empires?"

The yonat grunted. "That was what we expected. But what we actually found was planet after planet of dead land, drained of all its magic. Magic brings the life-spark every planet needs to thrive. If that magic is used up, the soul of the planet itself dies."

It was like Viera had been punched in the gut. She'd only just learned about magic, but she knew how painful it was to not have it. "They're planet killers? Can the planet be brought back to life?"

Flower Prancer's hoof scuffed the floor. "Not that we've seen."

"So, they came in and killed the planet that tried to sustain them. They killed their Mother ... well, not Earth, but mother none the less."

Thorn snarled, "And they're about to drain the soul of our planet past the point of saving if we don't move fast."

"It's a bit more complicated than that." Flower Prancer sounded stressed. Their ears twitched back. "Planets don't produce their own magic, though it is an integral part of their ecosystem."

"Of course they do," Thorn snapped. "It's why we all soak in magic when we're off-world, to replicate our planets' effects."

"No," Flower Prancer said simply. "Magic is produced by the living beings on a planet. The world can then amplify it and create a layer of magic we live and work in. Without us—beings with magic or *the potential* for magic—to give the initial seed, there is nothing to give life to the magical," the yonat clenched their jaw as if in thought, "blanket a planet produces that we're used to living in."

Thorn shook her head again. "But on Earth, that *blanket* is thick and potent."

"Well, there are the five pillars. Their magic is potent. All the humans have potential. Even if the planet isn't open for others to visit and take advantage of the magic, that is a lot of potential. With so few using it, it has done nothing but build up."

Viera's head hurt. "Stop. Hold up. There are magic users on Earth? Five of them?"

"Yes, dear, there have been for what you call years ... or, what did that beastly man call them? Centuries?"

"So, you're telling me ... like ... Is Merlin real? Or Gandalf? Or is it Harry Houdini or David Copperfield?"

Thorn slumped, sighing at the same time Flower Prancer's body visibly tensed. "That scallywag! One rule, there was one rule. Don't give away our secrets, and what does he do? He encourages a book be written. He becomes a muse. The jackal!"

Viera narrowed her eyes and gaped. "Wait, who's a jackal?"

"Why, Gandalf, of course. The others are made up or illusionists. It's obvious, isn't it? Think of the book." Flower Prancer's tail swished in irritation. "You are a bit slow, aren't you? Or is that all humans?"

As they spoke, Viera's jaw dropped open. "Wait, he's real? He's alive?"

Thorn reached over to rub her forearm. "Not anymore. He passed away a bit ago; his title and mantle shifted to a new pillar a few years ago."

"But in the book ... So, hobbits are real? And the elves? What other magical creatures am I going to be exposed to? Will I meet them?"

This elicited another grunt from Flower Prancer. "None. At least not from that blasted story. He made it all up. He wanted people to start thinking about magic, but not really knowing or understanding it."

Viera slumped. "None of it is real?"

"Well," the yonat bobbed their head back and forth as if they hated to give any credit to the scallywag. "The dwarves are real, but you'll probably never meet them. They've dedicated their lives to creating magically imbued items."

She thought about it, and realized she'd heard this part of the story before. "Like the GPS?"

"Yes, exactly. It's one of their greatest achievements, though they have others."

With a final gulp of coffee, Viera gazed at the two beings she was starting to think of as friends, though she wasn't sure how they saw her. "So, I create magic, but not enough to sustain myself off-planet, so I have to soak ... regularly. With others of my kind, we provide the planet's life-spark? And there are five magical people on Earth." Her head pounded. She needed a nap, and it wasn't even G-nine yet.

The horn bobbed up and down, dangerously close to her hurting head. "Yes. Now, we need to leave for the summit. One last thing. How many soaks did you do this morning?"

Viera blushed. "Two, why?"

"You glow, magically. One in the morning, one at night, or the magic sniffers are going to want to lick you."

And with that, the scary yonat and Thorn left the café.

The Good, The Bad, and The Ugly

Thorn

Thorn walked next to Flower Prancer as they made their way to the elevator. She shot a quick look over her shoulder at Viera. *She's adapting well, for a human ... so out of her depth here.*

The yonat shook his head. "What is it with humans and that horrible wizard? Every time I meet one, it's always Gandalf the Gray, then Gandalf the White, and eventually, 'Run, you fool!'"

Thorn chuckled. "I know you don't like the books, but have you lowered your standards to the point that you've watched the movies?"

"Why? It'd take half a day, and I have better things to do with my time." The scorn in his voice could cut a rock.

"Well, if you don't watch the movies, you'll never understand." She shrugged one shoulder. "It's not that important. It isn't like you'll be spending that much time with humans or on Earth. I'll be taking Viera home after the summit and that will be that. The five pillars are doing fine. I don't think they need you to visit."

His tail swished in irritation. "I haven't checked on them for a while; I may decide it's time." His voice sounded imperious.

As arrogant as his words were, putting Earth on his list of to-dos may mean any time in the next Earth decade or three. If Thorn won her arguments at the summit, she may not even be there to help with him and his ... attitude.

With a snarl, Flower Prancer asked, "Do the silly humans have other misconceptions?"

"Oh, so many." Thorn's eyes widened in anticipation. "Did you know that they think qynad are these huge mythological creatures called dragons that breathe fire? They are obsessed with them. There is a myth of a tall hairy man called Bigfoot that looks a lot like our fing."

Flower Prancer snorted. "Is that Toby? He's been hiding out on Earth for years."

Thorn covered her mouth. "I had no idea. You should give me his number. I'd love to see him after all these years. Does he know we're on planet?"

"Who knows with him? He's half-mad with his own self-imposed isolation. He's spent years avoiding all other creatures."

Thorn nodded, understanding that on a deep level. "There are a lot of stories that the Earthlings tell about creatures they think are made up. They always use different names. For weeks, Scout would come home from school in stitches. He'd show me his school papers with images. He told me the new names he'd learn. 'Look, Mom! It's a phoenix, not a tinder, although this picture looks a lot like my friend Axxi.'"

Flower Prancer's tail swished. "I'm not sure where these crazy names came from, but I'm guessing it was Gandalf and his ridiculous sense of humor."

As they reached the lift, she smirked at the yonat. "They have other mythological creatures. One of the ones that all young girls love are unicorns."

A low, menacing sound came from Flower Prancer. "When I was last on Earth, Gandalf told me of this creature."

"So, you know about them?"

"Yes, a horse with a horn, much like me."

Thorn nodded, trying to keep a blank face. "So, you know that white horses with rainbow hair and horns are every young girl's dream unicorn? They have a TV series based on this; they make cakes, dolls, shirts, everything."

His face snapped to her. "A series? Of what blasphemy do you speak?"

"There's a doll, Rainbow Brite, who rides a unicorn that looks like you. Different name."

The lift door opened and they both stepped in. "We won't speak of this again, Commander Firoza. Do you understand?"

Thorn bit her cheek to keep from laughing. The gruff and sometimes rude yonat was nothing like the kids' stories back on Earth. The idea he'd ever be friends with a young girl much less let a human ride him was ludicrous. "Yes, Elder."

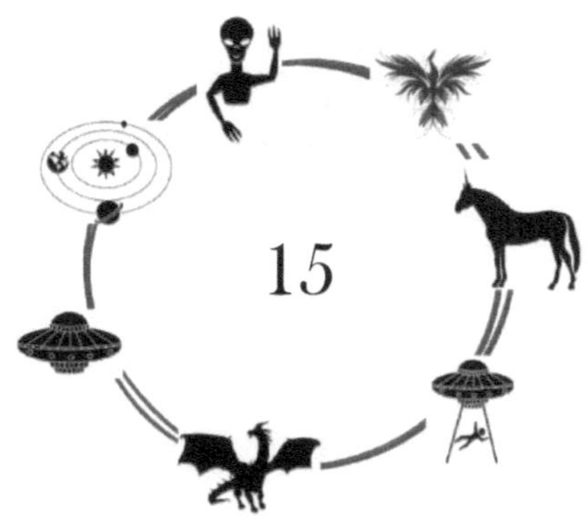

Glory Of The Yard

Viera

Back in the unit Viera shared with Thorn and Scout, Beaver ran over, leaping up, the ven's whole body vibrating with excitement.

"Are you hungry? I bet you're hungry. I wish I knew how to get you food. Maybe I can figure it out for a big, soft, furry, sweetie, moth-ball of cuteness."

Beaver's wings lifted from her side as Viera scratched behind her antenna and floppy ears. Odd purring sounds of contentment bubbled up from the pet's belly.

At the point Viera feared the animal's claws would pierce her pants and skin, she pushed down the over excited ven, and went to the panel by the table. "Um, computer thingy ... the, ah, ... Beaver, the ven, she's hungry and needs food."

Nothing happened and Viera sighed. She leaned against the wall and gazed down at the creature prancing around the room expecting the taller beast to take care of it. Viera tapped. "Hey, you, computer, food for Beaver."

There was a whirring sound, and a bowl appeared where her coffee had shown up the previous day. Beaver bounced on her front paws, ecstatic. Viera shook her head, annoyed and confused. *I have no idea what is going on.* She placed the bowl on the floor and let Beaver eat.

Once Beaver began scarfing, Viera sat on the couch and picked up her tablet, determined to learn ... something, anything. She'd barely gotten the device turned on when Scout bounded out of his room. "You're back! And my pesky pet convinced you she was starving. This is her second breakfast of the day. She's like a hobbit!"

"I've recently learned they aren't real. Wait, no. I've always known they aren't real, but I've learned *part* of that story is real." Viera went back to massaging her head. *How long until my head actually explodes? Maybe someone will get a recording and I can become the embodiment of the emoji. That'd be something at least.*

"Wanna go watch practice with me?" Scout bounced on his heels looking so hopeful that she knew this wasn't going to be a good idea.

"What are ... is ... practice?" She squinted at him, trying to lessen the motion he made.

"It's mostly the fings, but a few of the other groups join in ... maybe if we're lucky the qynad."

Viera held up a hand. "The big foot, or is it feet?, and the dragons, right?"

A smile took over his face. "That's it. The big creatures, unlike us, who are small and delicate."

"And are tasty with ketchup."

He snorted. "Anyway, they have practice drills and some competitions. They're open to the public to watch. We can go down and observe."

"Do they fight each other?"

"Not today. It's just a competition to destroy a wall. There will probably be betting, but we can avoid that. It's just fun to watch."

She looked down at the tablet, but decided the opportunity wouldn't present itself again ... ever ...

in her lifetime. Seeing a Bigfoot, or a dragon ... decimate a wall? How could she refuse?

As they walked to the lift and traveled down three levels, Viera wondered if they should've left Beaver behind, but as soon as the doors opened, she flew off to 'hang with her buds.' There were other ven as well as the phoenix-looking creatures and other flying beasts. They all sat in high branches on perches made for them.

She and Scout found a couple of seats that faced a large oval arena. It wasn't quite as big as a race car track, but close. In the center were two large walls. As she waited, giddy with excitement, all sorts of creatures and aliens filed in, filling in the space.

"Friends and Foe, Beasts and Burdens, Supports and Skeptics, welcome to the training yard. We have several rounds this morning and more after the midday meal. Each wall crumble will be fought in a side-by-side race, starting with Horax the Horrible."

Viera cheered with the rest of the crowd. She was excited to see the dragon with blue and green scales proudly enter the right side of the domed arena. She leaned down to Scout. "Did you know he'd be competing?"

"No! He only sometimes does, and I didn't know it was today."

The announcer continued in a booming baritone. "His competitor, Beau the Brave!"

For a moment, Viera was caught up on the name, expecting a beautiful human to walk out with thick corded muscles and maybe a magical hammer. Long dirty blond hair and sparkling eyes would search the crowd making everyone feel they were the person of interest. A few women would swoon and collapse in a fit.

Instead, a huge Bigfoot ... fing ... lumbered in holding a thick, spiked, club. His beady eyes glared at no one and everyone as he stomped to the center of his side and waited.

"The contestants have until at least seventy-five percent of their wall is down. They can use anything they brought into the arena with them, as well as anything they find. This is a battle-type scenario. Winner moves on to the next round, which takes place at G-sixteen. Time starts ... now."

Viera wanted to watch Horax, support him with her knowing his every move, but as soon as she realized he was heating the wall to make it soft, she shifted to see what Beau, the Not-So-Happy, did.

She expected him to run up with his weapon and begin to hack away, but instead he set down the weapon and started moving his hands in a pattern. She narrowed her eyes and searched his face. The big guy's lips moved but Viera couldn't hear what he said as he intently stared down the wall.

Not wanting to miss anything, Viera kept shifting her glance back and forth, keeping tabs on both competitors. Neither changed their starting move.

When she flicked her focus back to Beau, the big guy's fingers were spread wide, and it looked like he'd tensed every muscle in his body. Small cracks formed in the wall in front of him. The dome must've been soundproof, because she couldn't hear a thing.

She was so intent on those fissures, it wasn't until Scout tapped her leg that she saw Horax had dashed forward and spun, slamming his tail into the heated wall. As her jaw dropped, so did over half the bricks, crumbling on and around her friend. He flew up and jerked, spreading the mess around himself.

Once he landed, his tail went to work taking down more bricks.

A cry from those around her had her spinning her gaze towards Beau. His spiked club slammed into the wall, faster than she could easily follow. Though his wall was still over half up, each swing took down a massive chunk.

The race was on.

All around them, people screamed out their preferred winner. Others whispered out bets, money exchanging hands.

On their perches above, the birds and ven squawked and chittered away. The only thing that didn't make any sound were the walls being systematically destroyed.

Finally, a loud bell rang, and everyone froze. Viera looked around, then leaned down to Scout. "Who won?" To her, both walls looked similarly destroyed.

"I ... you know, I'm not sure. It's usually a lot easier to tell."

"This was an exciting one, don't you think?" the announcer's voice boomed out. "Both these competitors would do well in the next round, but unfortunately, we can only let one move on. So, who should it be? Our magic-wielding fing, with the sharp stick? Or our fire-breathing qynad whose tail I never want to run into in a dark valling."

Viera looked questioningly at Scout. He shrugged. "Similar to an alley, but more like a pit ... filled with villains."

"Ah, got it."

"But to get to what you all have been waiting for." Viera had wondered if he'd ever get to it, but while he spoke, the debris had been stacked on a floating platform. "Both competitors knocked the seventy-fifty percentage down in the same swipe. To get our final winner, we need to get a precise weight of what was knocked off the wall. This is a close one!"

Scout started to bounce. "It's never this close. To start off like this is good luck for the season. It's amazing! The planners are probably patting themselves on the backs."

Creatures came out with simple brooms and started to sweep up the mess. All bits were added to the floating platforms. Everyone that Viera saw sat at the edge of their seats, watching. After several minutes, the announcer finally returned. "The weights have been recorded. By point two percent, we have a winner."

There was a pause as boxes floated down in front of the platforms and started to flash some sort of symbols, she assumed it was numbers. This felt like every human reality show she'd ever seen. "And after this commercial break..." she whispered to herself.

The symbols stopped. Some people cheered and clapped while others grumbled and sighed. A few beat their firsts in the air. Scout smiled wide. She leaned down. "Horax won?"

His mouth dropped open. "I forgot you can't read anything here. Yes! He won! Let's go find him and take him to lunch."

Five Star ... Conversation

Viera

Scout led Viera through the crowds. Because the final call involved weighing the debris, the next fight would be starting soon; all they had to do was remove the rest of the standing walls and replace them with new walls. Apparently—according to the kid—it was easy-peasy.

Finding Horax was more difficult. They had to navigate to the training area and then were denied access. Viera wasn't upset about that. She really didn't want to see what happened in the locker rooms. She asked for a message to be delivered to Horax telling him they wanted to join him for the midday meal. She'd actually started off by saying 'lunch,' but only Scout knew what she meant, and he had to explain it to the attendant.

This was her second day on the space station. She reckoned she'd figure out about none of it right in time to head home. Then she'd have to not tell Betsy about it all.

Gah! She hadn't thought about Betsy at all. They were supposed to have a girls' night out on Tuesday. What day was it on Earth? Her watch had died without its normal charge cycle, as had her phone, so her connections to home were gone.

If her calculations were correct, it was still Monday, but she really wasn't sure.

The door to the trainer's area opened, and Horax lumbered out. "Heya, champ." He nose-butted Scout. "I hear we're having our midday meal, though it's still early." He focused on Viera. "Did you enjoy the show?"

"I did. I have so many questions ... I feel that's about all I've been doing since you all beamed me up, but alas, it's true."

"Well, I love questions, and Thorn isn't here to stop me from talking this time. Why don't we go up and find a quieter place to sit? You ask, I'll answer—or do my best."

She smiled. While this morning she felt like she *could* be friends with Flower Prancer, to her it felt like Horax had already crossed that divide.

She and Scout walked over to the lift, but there was an area on the far side of the station where creatures could stretch their wings. Beaver followed Horax after a few questioning bounces and squawks.

They met in the large domed area, teaming with beings of all shapes and sizes. Viera stopped trying to categorize them. Even the ones they'd told her about seemed to melt from her mind. The poor bit of her was so overwhelmed with each new piece of information. Despite that, she wanted to attempt to cram more in.

At the coffee shop where she'd dined with Thorn earlier, they sat at a side table with enough room for Horax to stretch out. The server dropped two menus before dashing to another table to help a group of six ... no, there was a small being tucked to the side. Seven.

Scout picked up his menu, scrunching up his face as he read the options. Horax tilted his large head to get a better view. Viera sat back and waited.

The server returned with an electronic pad. "Do you know what you want?"

Viera shrugged. "Sorry, no. I can't read the menu, I only read the language of my planet. Do you have suggestions?"

She sighed, face flattening in annoyance. Scout's expression tightened in her defense. "I'll help her decide. Give us some time. Horax will signal you."

The server's eyes fell on the dragon ... qynad. *Get this figured out, Viera, how hard can it be?* She beamed. "You won the first round. Meal's on the house."

Viera opened her mouth to object, when Horax's tail twitched. "I'll let you know when we're ready."

When she left, Horax sighed. "It was only the first round. It shouldn't matter. But the match was so evenly fought, it'll be discussed for ... well, too long." He blinked. "Have the Taco Tuesday special with a side of sushi," he suggested.

She shook her head in confusion. "Tacos and sushi?"

"Yeah, it's the Earth special. You can have a baked potato or potatoes au gratin with it."

With some difficulty, Viera bit back a laugh. "Okay, yeah. Sounds ... good."

After they ordered, Horax asked, "So, what are your questions?"

Viera considered. "This morning I met Flower Prancer."

Both Scout and Horax jerked as if this were big news. Horax leaned in towards her. "One of the yonat came out and he spoke with you?"

"Is that ... wrong?" I made a mental note that Horax called Flower Prancer a 'he.'

"No, it's just that the Elders usually stay out of the day-to-day grind. That's half the reason for the summit—-asking them to pay attention to what's happening and help. If they step in, the krottel will have to listen."

Scout squirmed in his seat. "I'm sorry, Ms. Kor, I've been messing up. I never told you about the bad guys."

She reached down and squeezed the boy's hand. "It's okay, Scout. I've gotten most of the story from your mom and Flower Prancer. They told me about the krottel and how they invaded your planet. The yonat are trying to figure out the truth behind everybody's stories."

Horax nodded. "Okay, then what can I help you with?"

"In the arena, your competitor, Beau, he used magic, right?"

"Well, now, I couldn't see him. We're blocked from viewing each other." Viera slumped down in her chair, disappointed. "But I did catch a bit in a replay. I plan to watch the full challenge tonight."

Excitement bubbling up in her, Viera sat forward in her seat. "So, magic?"

"Yes," Horax confirmed. "He used magic while I used fire ... magic-enhanced fire."

"Oh! You used magic, too."

"It's fairly common in the arena. It's another reason I need food before the next match. It drains one's own personal power to use magic."

Now Viera got to what she felt was important. "Does everyone use magic? Have magic? Am I the only one not magical?" She felt very plebeian. She had nothing, no magic, no abilities, hell, she couldn't even read or tell who won a silly competition.

"Everyone has the potential to do magic, and most people here can tap in to do a little, but no, not everyone is magical. Are you feeling left out?" Horax tilted his head at her.

His astute question made her feel seen, but not in the best of ways. She wanted people here to think of her as strong and well-balanced.

"I can do magic!" Scout beamed. "I can look like a lot of different beings." His outburst caused Beaver to dance in her spot. Then she looked around as if searching for a party.

The server took that moment to bring them their food. Beaver dashed over to 'help' her. Viera's quick distraction, petting the soft head and scratching down the neck, was the only thing that stopped the beast from attacking the server for what she carried.

Horax slurped up some of his food as Viera tried a taco. It surprised her that it tasted good, not quite like something found on Earth, but it made her feel a bit grounded. The sushi roll likewise was decent.

"Where does the fish come from?"

Horax made a sound like rocks grinding together. Viera realized he laughed at her. "We are orbiting near a planet."

At least she wasn't worried about getting sick.

"Most beings only do one of two spells—the magics of their people. Like Scout; all of his people can change their appearance at will." The qynad smiled at Scout, giving the young boy a wink.

"Some beings can do spells and mix potions," Horax continued. "My opponent was closer to the latter. He probably couldn't mix up a concoction, but he could do several defensive and offensive spells."

As she listened, Viera imagined what it would be like to throw spells around, just for shits and giggles.

17

The Enemy of My Friend Is My Enemy

Viera

"Is there any way I can learn magic?" Viera asked. "Or is it always going to be out of reach?"

Horax's tail twitched. Throughout his lecture, everything about magic had been theoretical. She'd just turned the tables on him. "You have to understand, magic is something inside you, like your beating heart. A part of you that you can manipulate, like your hand."

Between them, Beaver pushed her bowl of food, banging it into Viera's foot. She reached down to scratch the ven.

"But I soaked in magic this morning. Don't I have these magical feelers ... finders within me which I can use to ... I don't know, do things with?" Viera waved her hands about. She wasn't sure how far she could take the analogy, but she now imagined magical tentacles floating from her body, ready to play catch or slap away a bad guy ... not that there *were* villains in her life to beat on.

The qynad got visibly agitated as his tail began to twitch and his voice grew tighter. "Viera, it's more complicated than that. Though your body is used to surviving in the ocean of magic your planet is saturated in, you yourself are not magical. You aren't a wizard." His tail snapped back and forth. "Your planet's magic layer is one of the thickest I've ever experienced. It's a wonder only five humans have tapped into the part of you that allows a being to become a wizard, but humans are very shut against the possibility of magic. At this point, the five pillars are it. They have been standing strong for as long as I can remember."

Disappointment filled Viera. A fleeting thought of standing over a cauldron, wearing a black cape and a pointy black cap flitted through her head. *Bubble and toil, with this spell the krottel's plan will foil.* She shook her head and smiled warily. "Okay, I can't perform magic, but could I mix magical potions? Make concoctions? Become a spell-master?" She imagined herself over a huge black pot with the scent of frankincense filling her small kitchen.

Horax snorted and a bit of smoke billowed from his snout. "You need to be magical to do any kind of magic, child."

How old is he that I'm a child to him?

Viera scrunched up her face, trying to remember the books she'd read so long ago. "I know I was told that Gandalf lied when he inspired the *Lord Of The Ring* books, but in those books there were only five wizards on Earth, right?"

Scout bounced in his seat. "In every fable there exists a core of truth. It's how we learn from even the most outlandish stories."

At Scout's excitement, Beaver darted from under the table, flying up to sit with the other flying creatures. Viera watched as Beaver rubbed faces with a family of phoenixes.

With a sigh, Viera stared down at the boy. "Do you listen to all my lessons so closely?"

"Of course! You're an amazing teacher. That's why I gave you that mug." His wide smile was infectious, and she smiled back at him.

"The mug that landed me here." She waved a hand around, indicating the space station. She wasn't completely disappointed in the way things had turned out. "You know, I'm starting to understand your reactions to my mythical creatures lesson last winter. I'm explaining why dragons aren't real, and you're just looking forward to watching Horax's competitions."

Horax's head jerked up and he gazed at the wall as Scout giggled. Then the dragon-looking being settled back down. "To answer your question, no, you can't just learn magic or potions or any of it. You have magic in you—we all do—but without the spark of what you call *the wizard* you can't perform the magical arts. The five pillars have protected your world for generations. For some reason, magic slows the aging in you humans once you hit the age of—" He stopped talking, looking around the room.

Next to her Scout said, "It's twenty-five, or so, Horax. That's when aging slows. More than my people ... I think. Mom said, for human wizards, it's like they live forever."

With a twitch of his tail, Horax continued. "Right. After that, those with the spark stop visibly aging and begin their work. The pillars have known about our kind, especially the Elders, for ..." he said a word the translator didn't translate. The sound that came from his large mouth sounded like rocks rubbing together. "A long time. This is getting into a level of history I don't know. You'd have to ask the wizards—*if* you can find them. There's probably one near Scout's settlement, but they're pretty busy."

Scout smiled. "Busy, but *our* wizard is really bad at card games. I win all the time. Oh, and at chess. But I'm good at different games."

He swung his gaze to Scout, eyes softened. "That you are, my boy, very good at games. That you are."

"Is the wizard famous? Would I know him?" Viera asked.

Scout laughed and Horax's head moved slightly. "No. All the pillars stay under the radar. There's very little chance you know any of the five. Now, I need to prepare for the next round. I'll see you both there? It'll be in about an hour."

Scout beamed and exclaimed, "Yes!"

Once the qynad left, Viera told the server to put the meal on Thorn's account, and she and Scout moved to a table in the center of the promenade.

Narrowing his eyes, Scout asked, "Do you want to play chess? I'll take it easy on you."

Viera looked around at the crowds. One of the aliens sent a shiver down her spine. She realized she hadn't seen that one before. With a slight tilt and nod, she indicated the one. "What is that?"

It moved around like it floated, no bouncing step, no flowing gait. None of the other creatures blocked its path; they all shifted to give the ominous being space.

It wore a dark navy-blue cloak lined in a light gray fur that covered it past its feet. The cloak itself was embroidered in a geometric pattern and the hood was up. The alien wore a light cerulean mask over its face with no adornment. Black gloves covered its hands. *Why does this alien want to cover all its skin? Is it sensitive to light, like a vampire?*

Viera kept looking back and forth between the alien and Scout, expecting some proclamation of species, but he sat with his face scrunched up in fury, hands fisted, green eyes glaring daggers. She didn't want an intergalactic incident. "Scout, talk to me."

As his ire built, Beaver flew down, curling in around Scout's feet, the ven apparently responding to Scout's emotion. *That animal is amazing.*

The boy slowly turned, fire in his young face. "Sorry, Ms. Kor." He closed his eyes for a moment and took several deep breaths before continuing. "I didn't expect to see any of them, especially on the promenade. They don't usually come around people. It's one of the krottel, the people that invaded my planet."

Checkmate

Viera

Viera watched the krottel as it appeared to glide—or float—across the promenade.

She wrapped her arm around Scout. "Hey, it'll be okay, it's not coming this way. The space station's safe, right?"

"Yeah, I guess. I just ... I don't like them, Ms. Kor." He kept watching the krottel.

Viera realized most of the other aliens were treating the krottel in a similar fashion as Scout. None of the different beings seemed to be welcoming of the oddly floating creature. Beyond giving them a wide berth, many seemed tense. Viera saw twitching tails and fluffed feathers.

I wonder if the krottel feels rejected by this treatment?

As the path closed behind the cloaked figure, Viera eventually lost sight of it. She gave Scout a friendly shake and turned him back to the table. "Okay, smart kid, what about that chess match? You think you can beat me? Your teacher? Your number one teacher in all of the galaxy?"

He giggled, finally breaking out of the nervous, angry stupor he'd gotten into seeing the hated foe that'd invaded his world.

He tilted his head, the dark purple hair flopping over. "I know I can win, but in the spirit of our day of competition, let's make this a real competition with prizes."

"Why do I feel like you set me up, kiddo?"

His eyes twinkled. Next to him, Beaver wiggled. Scout dropped his hand to pet his friend then he looked at her. "Go, Beaver. Find your friends. Fly while you have the chance."

His gaze shifted to Viera. "Back on Earth, she can't fly very much. If anyone caught sight of her in the air, they'd freak out. We can let her do a bit of flying at night, but there are so many cameras and drones, it just isn't very safe."

Viera leaned back. "What about an indoor gymnasium? Why don't your people build something like that? You could exercise, let your pets fly. If you like to swim, you could add a pool. I don't know if your way of exercising is the same as ours, but if it isn't, it'd allow for anonymity while training."

Scout made a funny face when his arms flopped to the sides like wet noodles. "I don't know. I just go to school and play with kids my size. The rest is up to my mom and cousins and other adults."

Viera had been gone from Earth for ... three days? Maybe four days? With the thirty-hour clock and time on the space station off from home, she wasn't really sure. But it suddenly occurred to her, besides magic, there was a plethora of questions she hadn't asked.

"Scout, how many of your people live on Earth?"

"A lot? There are something like fifty settlements all over the place."

Her head was about to explode, this time for real. "How many people in each settlement?"

He shrugged. "I don't know. Mom said more than in the school, but not enough to change the census... does that make sense to you?"

"Our school? The elementary school?" That wasn't too bad, a few hundred per group.

"I think she meant the school where my cousin works. The college ... the one in Whitewater."

Viera opened her mouth, then shut it again. She thought about that. It wasn't the flagship university, but it probably had between ten and twenty thousand ... *thousand* ... students. That, times fifty ... a million of them were on Earth? She rubbed her head.

Her mouth was getting dry. How could one planet take on a million refugees and not even know it? But, then again, how could they turn them away? The chanzii needed to go somewhere. Gah! This was so hard.

Scout started tapping on the table. Viera realized it was one of the panels. A few moments later, a holographic chess board appeared between them.

"So, Ms. Kor, if I win, tonight you read to me any book I choose, even if you think it's too adult for me. You have to remember I'm older than I look."

She narrowed her eyes. "What book do you want me to read you?"

"Wyldling Snare by A.R. Grimes. It's one of my favorites."

She happened to like the book too, and it was definitely not too mature for him. There was a fight scene in it, but she loved that book for him.

"What if *I* win?" Her eyebrow rose in challenge.

He gave her his most mischievous grin. "Then *I* read the book to you!"

Happiness bubbled within her. This was one of the reasons he was one of her favorite students. He just brought her so much joy. "It's a deal."

The game started, and they seemed to be evenly matched. It went against everything in her to let a kid win. They didn't learn any good lessons by being given a free pass. That didn't mean she played her best game, but she did play well.

Halfway through the game, he paused. "I'm thirsty, how about you?"

"I could use a drink."

"Good. I'll go get us something, you hold the table." He narrowed his eyes and pointed at her. "No cheating!"

She laughed as he slipped away. While she waited she looked up to find Beaver. She sat with two other moth-pets. There seemed to be a lot of ven at the station. There were a few other groups in the tree branches dotting the ceiling.

I wonder if they've spayed or neutered, or have done the equivalent ... or if that's a thing. Or how cute are the moth-ven babies?! She suddenly wanted a pack of them tumbling around her living room.

When Scout returned, he had a chocolate shake and a vanilla shake. "Which flavor do you want? I like them both. I mean, everyone loves chocolate more, but I like any kind of shake, really." A huge smile was plastered on his face as he held them out.

"For the record, boyo, this isn't something to drink." She gave him a fake scowl, then took the vanilla. She preferred chocolate—he was right about that—but she could tell he really wanted it.

He laughed as he looked at the board and took his turn. She was happy the shake tasted mostly as she expected. There was a bit of an odd flavor, but she decided she'd learned enough new things for one week, and just moved her piece. Scout sighed at her move and took his turn.

They continued until she won. "Best of three?"

It had been close. He hadn't been wrong when he'd said he was a good player. "Sure."

The second game seemed to go faster. Scout had loosened up and had a plan. Viera had noticed the krottel reappear on the opposite side of the promenade and had been distracted. *Is that the same one? Do they all dress the same? Are they humanoid under the mask, cloak, and gloves? If so, why hide? Do they just have really sensitive skin?*

"Checkmate!" Scout called out. "Were you even trying Ms. Kor?"

"I'm sorry. I was, but with all the aliens in the room, it's so fascinating."

Scout searched the different creatures but the krottel had already disappeared in the crowd. Thankfully, he didn't see it. He shrugged. "Yeah, I guess I'm used to them. Any you want to ask about?"

Her head swam. *Any? All of them.* Over the first day and a half she'd only really focused on the ones whose shapes she recognized from Earth tales. There were so many more. But she already struggled. "Yes and no. Like you, my sweet student, I want to learn it all, but right now there is just too much to learn for me to actually remember. I think I'm close to capacity for this trip. The aliens that remind me of the beasts of legend from Earth. It's as good a place to start as any."

Scout nodded. "You've learned a lot, Ms. Kor, you're doing a really good job. Maybe not at chess, but at other things."

She chuckled. "Why, thank you."

He looked down at his empty shake container. "Want something to drink?"

She narrowed her eyes. "Are you angling for another shake?"

"No, a real drink this time, like water or milk."

She sighed. "Then yes, I'd love something to drink. Nothing sweet."

"Got it!" He took her glass and ran off to get another round.

She watched him until the crowd swallowed him up. She let her gaze slide over the myriad of shapes and sizes of creatures in the room. Some were furry, some had scales, some lumbered while some flew. There was so much in the galaxy to learn, and she knew it was more than she had time to absorb in her lifetime.

She turned back to where Scout disappeared when a pain on the back of her head startled her. Then everything went black.

19

Magic Doesn't Mean Disappearing

Scout

"I would like two glasses of water, please." Scout smiled at the fing who ran the shop. He knew Bob and figured he'd be the easiest shop owner to visit.

"Scout, I'm working, you can't just barge in my store every time you want something. There's a cafe across the way for things like water." The tall, hairy creature sneered down at him.

Undaunted, Scout smiled. "But Mom said to trust you. You know there's a lot of creatures around The Center, and not all will talk to kids. You know Mom and know she's good for the bill.

Horax is off at the practice fields, so he can't go to the shops with me. That leaves you." He smiled again, opening his eyes wide. He tried to look as much like Beaver as he could; that ven of his was the cutest thing he knew.

Bob glared. "When you grow up, boy, you go into politics, just like your mom. You want water?"

"I want a water. I'm also getting something for Ms. Kor, my teacher."

The big fing rolled his eyes. "Two waters coming up, and I'm putting it on a bill. Your mom *will* be paying up, young Scout."

"Yes, sir!"

It took the larger creature only a few minutes to gather two glasses of water, and he smiled when he bent to hand them to Scout. Once his hands were free, he gave Beaver a pet. Scout knew most of Bob's grousing was all for show.

"Okay, Beaver, back up to the trees with you. There are too many people milling about. Watch from above."

Scout knew Mom liked having an extra pair of eyes on him. Though the ven couldn't communicate with words, if anything happened to him, the ven would fight to help Scout, or follow whoever took him. Then Beaver would find Mom and lead her to Scout. She was an amazing companion.

When he got to the table, Ms. Kor wasn't there. *She must've had to go to the restroom. We've been playing for a while.*

Scout put Ms. Kor's glass down on the table and found a game to play while he waited. Over the intercom, they announced the start of the Practice Field Competitions. Horax wasn't in the first round, but Scout did a quick search for Ms. Kor. *I really want to get down there. All the competitions are fun to watch.*

He finished his game and checked the time. It had been almost twenty minutes since he sat down.

Scout scrunched up his face. *Ms. Kor can't use the space port computers, so she can't leave me a message, but if she'd gone to the restroom, how long would it take? Would she know where to go up here? She'd probably go to our rooms.*

Decision made, he started back to the rooms. When he got there, she wasn't in the main room. "Ms. Kor! Are you here? It's me, Scout, looking for you."

He slowly entered her room, but she wasn't lying in bed. With some trepidation, he even checked her private restroom. Nothing.

Could she be in my room or Mom's? He started to feel like Goldilocks with the three bears. He giggled at the analogy but continued to search.

His heart started to pound faster, and his palms got wet. "Where is she, Beaver? Where could she have gone? Would she have gone to the practice fields without me? That doesn't make sense, does it?"

His mind raced. *Maybe she returned to the game table, but I was gone and now she's worried about me. No, that doesn't make sense. I don't think she would've left in the first place. Shopping? There are all the shops and Mom said she could use her name as credit ... but why go without me? Should I go check each of the shops? Does that make sense? Would one of the other aliens have lured her away? Like the stupid krottel? Maybe they saw her sitting with me and want to explain their side to her. Like, they think she has Mom's ear. That makes sense.* He shook his head. Nothing made sense.

He stared down at his hands. Beaver jumped up on the couch and nudged him for some pets. Scout gave the ven the attention she craved, soothing both of them. "I know, I know, you're right." Though his belly felt like it was doing somersaults, he finally came to a decision. "I have to contact Mom. She's always told me it was my duty as a son to let her know when things weren't right. Ms. Kor was my responsibility, and I don't know where she is."

Beaver made a sound that sounded suspiciously like approval. He debated calling Juniper, or someone else from the ship, but in the end, he got up and sent a signal to his mom.

Back on the couch, he wrapped his arms around his legs and placed his chin on his knees. Curled in a ball, he rocked slightly. He swallowed hard, trying to stop himself from crying. Everything felt wrong. Ms. Kor wasn't supposed to be missing on the space station, she was supposed to be back on Earth, safe.

He pushed Beaver away. "I don't deserve your snuggles; this is all my fault."

20

How Many Times Will We End Up Not In Kansas?

Viera

Viera's head pounded. Her body felt cramped. *Did I sleep wrong?* She realized she was on her back. *I never sleep on my back. What the hell is going on?*

She tried to rub her throbbing forehead with her right hand. It stopped moving with a clink and she realized a heavy weight hung from her wrist. Her eyes snapped open, but the room was dark. Her left hand stopped its path just as abruptly. Both her legs were secured as well.

Her breathing started to get ragged.

A tremble started in her hands, traveled up her arms, and hit her body, matching the thumping of her heart in her chest.

What's happened? Where am I?

She tried to trace back to what she'd been doing before she woke up strapped down. She didn't think this had to do with anything sexy or fun.

Playing back anything she could remember, the image of a big foot spewing magic with a bludgeoning device flashed through her head. Then a knight took her king. A vanilla shake. Ven canoodling in the trees and their babies playing in her living room back home.

Viera shook her head. *My silly memories are suspect. Not all of these things happened. I did play chess. But then ... gah! That pain. Did someone hit my head?*

She tried to sit up as her mind caught up with her day but slammed back down because of the restraints. *What happened to Scout? Is he still on the promenade? Is he okay?*

Her pain took a backseat to the fear she felt for the innocent boy. *Did whoever take me take him too?* A lump of fear knocked into her as she worried about him. *Please let him be okay.* She didn't know who she asked ... the universe? She wasn't religious, but she needed him to be safe.

Viera, calm down. Freaking out right now won't help you. It won't help Scout. It won't help anything. You need to be ready when the people who took you come back.

Taking a shaky breath, Viera forced herself to relax. When her class got wild, she did a form of meditation with them to calm them down. She made a game of it. Now, with her mind spinning like a whirling dervish, she had to play that game with herself. Anything to save her energy.

Once she soothed away the frantic jitters, she thought about her situation. *How long have I been here? Does Thorn know I'm missing? Am I still on the space station?*

Nope, she couldn't go down *that* route. Imagining being nabbed by some alien, taken away to a new place, and never being found again was beyond her right then. She had to focus on getting away, being rescued, returning to Earth in a few days. It may not be true, but for now it was what she needed.

She started twisting and tugging at her right wrist. There was a bit of movement but no give to the cuff. She could extend her arm just far enough that she didn't have leverage to yank or tug to try to get her hand free.

There was similar give with her feet. *For fuck's sake!*

The only thing left to do was rest and wait until her head stopped pounding. Maybe then she could come up with something clever.

When Viera opened her eyes, she flinched at the light. She immediately closed her eyes before slowly slitting them open, allowing them to adjust to the brightness of the room.

Being able to see where she was didn't help. The straps secured her to a platform slightly tilted with her feet down. The white walls reflected the light like fresh snow. And she had to go to the bathroom. None of this improved her headache.

Once she could fully open her eyes, she searched the area, but it didn't help. A fully whitewashed room didn't have many secrets to tell. One wall had a door. It was closed. She was pretty proud of her detective work considering her headache.

With a sigh, she laid her head back down to wait. She couldn't fathom why someone would go to the trouble to take her or all people, but then, once they had her, just leave her. It all seemed ... ridiculous.

Please tell me we're still on Torville Station Number Six. And what a funny name for a space station. She wanted to admonish herself to focus, stay on task, but really, what else did she have to do?

From behind her came a click. She jerked her head in the direction of the door and saw it starting to open. For some reason, seeing one of the krottel glide in wasn't as surprising as it should've been. She had no idea why the invading alien wanted her, but the creepy being obviously did.

It came to stand next to her, its mask hiding where it looked. "Human," its voice came out in a monotone, "you will tell me where your planet is."

21

Ever Feel Like You've Been Bugged?

Viera

The creature that stood over her looked humanoid. It stood maybe six, six and a half feet tall. The cape or jacket it wore fell column straight, so whatever body it covered was rail thin. Whatever it was gave Viera the heebie-jeebies. A shiver ran down her spine.

She squeezed her eyes shut then opened them. *What is it hiding? Is it so hideous it fears my reaction?*

Her mouth suddenly was as dry as any desert back home. "How long have I been here? Are there restroom facilities? Do I get one phone call?"

The krottel didn't move. After a few seconds it repeated itself. "Human, you will tell me where your planet is."

Viera let her head fall back onto the platform. Part of her worried the krottel could hear her heart because it was beating so hard. Another part worried about her head. The pain had evolved into a splitting migraine. For some reason, she'd forgotten to pack her meds before coming on this trip. And the bright lights and spooky alien were *not* helping.

Finally, Viera let out her breath. "So, that's a 'no' on the restroom? I really need to go, and I'd hate to mess up your very clean jail cell. It's so bright and white in here."

"There's an automatic cleaning system." The monotone redoubled the spooky factor.

"What about my clothes? Are you expecting me to sit around in wet pants?"

The disturbing being backed up a bit, as if consulting someone, but Viera wasn't sure who or how. She couldn't hear anything and there was only one of the creatures in the room. "It has been decided. You can leave the security of this table and use the facilities if we can place one of our pet bugs on the back of your neck.”

“What?” Terror shivers surged through her. “A bug? It’ll crawl all over me. That’s creepy.”

“No, it will stay exactly where it is placed. If you have any ill intentions towards the krottel or try to escape, then it will bite you. In no other situation are you in danger.”

“Is this some sort of magic?” She couldn’t help the lilt of awe in her voice.

“Isn’t everything? It’s the glue that binds us all.” Between the monotonic way the creature spoke, the cadence, and the words it chose, Viera wondered if they were having the same conversation.

“So,” she said slowly. “You want me to allow a magical bug to ride on the back of my neck to the loo?”

“Correct.” Did Viera detect a hint of mockery in the alien’s voice?

She sighed. “And if I do or think anything negative or about escape, it’ll bite me.”

“Correct.” *Oh! I heard it that time! Exasperation!*

"And the bite will make me sick? Itchy? A weird infection?" None of this conversation helped her pounding head.

"Instant death."

Viera froze, the light air of the conversation, which really had been anything *but* light, suddenly took a very serious turn. If she could've, she'd have rubbed her eyes, or throbbing head. "You want me to allow a bug, whose bite will instantly kill me, to ride on the back of my neck?"

"Correct."

She could've throttled the krottel if it allowed her any movement. "Who does that?"

After a wait that went on for too long, the being said, "It won't happen by accident, if that's what you're worried about."

"Oh? And what if I drop my head back to stretch, forgetting the death bug is there?" she snapped at the jailer who wanted to so cavalierly take her life at a supposedly magical bug's discretion.

"It'll move. It's smart. It is of our world, not yours. On our planet, bugs are intelligent, revered." There was a softness to its monotone when it spoke of the creature.

"If you are so keen on the bugs of your world, why are you taking over others?"

It glided back up to the bed. "Are you taking the bug or are we continuing our conversation?"

At the start, she didn't really have to use the restroom very badly. Now it was more emergent. But all the discussion on skipping to the loo changed that. Now she felt that she only had a choice of location. Frustration bubbled within her. "You swear that damn thing won't just bite me? I'd really hate to get a death bite just because I have to pee."

Viera squeezed her eyes shut and when they opened an iridescent-green, ridged bug stood on the gloved hand of the alien. It had violet-blue, gold-edged wings, and the body had two parts, three if you included the small head. The six furry legs were a coppery gold, and the bug itself was small, maybe just under an inch.

I bet these aliens use the metric system ... two centimeters in length. And the bugger stands just about a half a centimeter tall. She shivered. It looked like some sort of beetle, and not the ones that stole the hearts of the world singing songs all those years ago.

The krottel moved slowly, as if not to scare her ... scare her more? ... and placed the thing on her shoulder. She shivered as it scurried to the back of her neck. Afterwards, her restraints were removed.

The alien led Viera through the door. The hallway was as white and sterile as the room. There weren't any other of the creatures milling about. They turned right and walked. Well, Viera walked; the krottel continued to glide. They passed a few cross passageways. All were as indistinct as the one they were in.

Though Viera noted some seams that could be doors, she didn't see any panels that would act in any way as an entry scanner. There weren't any computer displays. Everything was the same high-gloss white that covered the walls of the room she'd woken up in—her jail.

Eventually the hall ended in a T-intersection, and they turned right again. *It's like the shell of a video game or cartoon without any of the details. Even if I wanted to escape, how could I? Everything is the same. It's worse than a repeating background, there's no background.*

They took a turn to the left and then another turn. They got to a door, and it swung open. It looked like the restroom attached to her rooms with Thorn and Scout.

"You can use the facilities."

Is this the only one on the ship? Because Viera was convinced she was on the krottel ship. Whether or not they were still docked at Torville Station Number Six was a completely different question.

Once the door closed behind her, she saw that the small white room had a toilet and a sink. No shower. If she stayed too long, she wouldn't be able to soak in magic.

And then what would happen to her body once it lost all its residual power?

Even If You Say Please .. The Answer Is No

Viera

Before the long walk back to the room where they'd been holding her, Viera wondered if the alien had walked her in circles to mess with her. After the long walk, she debated if any of them ever had to use the toilet. She made a bet with herself that there was only one toilet on the whole damned ship, and how long the line was in the morning.

When they finally made it back to her holding room—at least, she thought it was the same room— they'd changed it. Instead of a platform bed with restraints, there was a table with food and drink at one end. *Oh, great, I'll have to use the facilities again; just what everyone wants!*

Viera took two steps into the room, then stopped. She assumed the food was for her, but every geometry student learning formal proofs knew what happened when you assumed.

"Sit, human, eat."

One of her eyebrows dashed up her forehead. "And how do I know the food is safe?"

"Why would we keep you alive this long only to poison you?"

That was ... not as comforting as it should've been. "Do you know what kinds of food I can eat?" It didn't smell bad. It smelled sweet, like syrup. There was a silver dome over the plate, so she couldn't see what they'd brought, but it didn't smell bad.

"The Earth breakfast special was ordered for you. It is popular with many of the aliens on the space station. We assume it is safe for you to eat."

A knot of tension hit Viera's belly as she made herself walk towards the table. "Breakfast?"

"Is that not a human meal? Stopping the fast of not eating?" The krottel sounded confused. "You were asleep and now awake. There was a fast, was there not?"

"How long have I been here?" She rested her hands on the table as she tried to get her breathing under control. *Is it day three? We're still at the station, but are Thorn and Scout still here? Would they leave without me? Will I ever see Earth again?*

"Please sit and eat."

A shiver traveled down her back. Viera sat and removed the cloche from her food. The plate had pancakes, sausage, fried eggs, and hash browns. She wondered what sort of eggs they were. Then she wondered about a lot of the ingredients that made her food. Next to her plate was a mug of coffee.

Her gut churned with worry about Scout and home and her future. The thought of all the sweet and heavy food made her queasy. "Why won't you tell me how long I've been here? I had been playing a game with a young boy ... Did you hurt him?" *Again,* she thought to herself, hoping they couldn't pick up on her thoughts. "And you feed me breakfast food. Is it morning?"

There was silence as Viera gazed at the food and the krottel stood. It looked ... real, but nothing else felt tangible. She just slowly breathed. *I don't have that odd feeling in me, so maybe it's still night?*

"If you don't want to eat, human, we'll talk. The food will be taken away."

Viera swallowed. Her hand trembled as she reached for the fork. "I'm eating."

The food tasted like the diner downtown back home on Earth. It was good. The pancakes were sweet and had a dollop of butter on them. The sausage and eggs were greasy, but there were hashbrowns to help sop up all the good bits. In the end, she went for the coffee. It made her feel centered, thinking of home and eating the familiar meal.

She tried not to think of the ominous person standing over her in a black cap and nondescript mask.

When she finished, she put the fork down and shut her eyes, focusing on questions she could ask. She didn't expect answers, but preparation was half the battle.

Opening her eyes, she saw a second alien cape flutter out the door just before it clicked shut. *Damn, I should've watched. I've only seen Mr. Happy here ... or is he a she? Ms. Fun and Games?*

Viera took a bracing breath and fake smiled. "So, why don't you join me at the table? You're always standing. Does it hurt your feet? I mean, all day clomping around, you must have amazing shoes."

"Tell me human, where is your planet?"

Her head started to pound. It was back to this.

"You know, you've asked one question, over and over, yet you've never answered any of mine."

"It is not the morning. You've been our humble guest for just over three hours. Where is your planet?"

"Guest? You knocked me out and tied me down to a platform. In what galaxy is that treating a person like a guest?"

There was a moment of pause. "Once you awoke, we released you. You have been fed. You are well, are you not?"

She thought about that. The alien wasn't wrong. After the initial take down, they hadn't treated her poorly, but she didn't feel magnanimous enough to say so. "I don't know how to answer your question. Why do you want it anyway?"

"We need your magic. We heard the qynad and the yonat tell you there was a thick layer of magic on your planet. We need that."

She shook her head. "My people aren't like the chanzii. They won't up and leave; they'll fight. There are billions of humans on my planet and each and every one of them will fight."

Again, the krottel seemed to think about her words. Viera wasn't sure why. She was one human, it was one ... something. One of whatever they were. *Why isn't this discussion happening on a larger scale?*

"Your people will wise up and leave when they realize survival is only possible elsewhere."

"No," Viera said with a sad finality. The krottel glided back as if struck.

"Why are you so certain, human?"

"My people have no place to go. We haven't learned about interstellar, much less intergalactic flight. The idea of aliens will freak out most of the humans beyond normal fears. They will fight." As she spoke, she realized the truth in her words. Though she wanted to scare off this alien, this planet-killer, the words brought her a deep, gut sadness. Her people weren't ready for all she'd learned and experienced there the last few days. As wonderful as it may have been.

"My species have no way of telling if you speak the truth. Not on the surface. I am sorry, human, but we need to learn if you are protecting us or your world."

As the words sank in, she felt a pinch high up on her back, just below her shoulders, over her spine. It took her a moment to piece together what the sting meant, what it could be, then heat flooded her system.

Images from Earth flashed through her mind: war, battle, people scared, the things she'd just been thinking. Interspersed were flashes of her parents' faces, Betsy, her best friend, her school, her students. It became too much. They were taking her thoughts.

And was the bite ... fatal? With a yowl of fear and anger, she yelled, "No!"

23

There Is No Pain You Are Receiving

Viera

"No!" The word echoed through the room as it ripped out of Viera, mind, body, and soul. She'd meant the word with every fiber of her being. It meant more than the negation—of not wanting to die—it was her hating that they'd seen people and places she loved through her memories. Somehow, by allowing their pet bug to bite her, they'd taken a piece of her.

As she screamed out the word, she stood, and flung her arms out wide. The heat that had been building inside her, burning her, boiling within her, had to find an escape.

Like a volcanic explosion, it released from her body. Her 'no' morphed into a scream of triumph as all the rage shot out of her.

Viera watched, as if in slow motion, as her power slammed into the being standing watch over her. It started with the cloak billowing open, but what she saw made no sense: the black lines of a kid's scribbled out drawing.

Then as if an explosion were happening outside her body as large as what she felt inside, the krottel flew everywhere, raining out around the room in thousands of tiny iridescent bits. The cape slowly billowed to the ground, the mask fell with a crash, and Viera thought her heart would stop.

Taking a step back, Viera watched in disgusting fascination and horror as bugs, similar to the one that bit her, scurried all around the floor. Thousands of them. They all aimed for one that was ... bigger. It had a shape similar to theirs, but instead of being two centimeters in length it was probably half a foot long. It stood its ground, glaring at Viera.

"What did you do to us?" The voice reverberated in the room.

Viera sputtered. *The bug talks?* "Me? What did I do to you? What the fuck did you do to me? You told me the bite from that bug would kill me instantly. And when it bit, me it tried to steal my memories." She knew she spit out the words, but the anger still simmered deep within her.

"We bit you to see if you lied about your world. Your memories are safe with you. Our magic is very limited, that is why you knew we watched your thoughts."

Viera shook her head. "You didn't bite me, one of the smaller bugs did. I'd be truly dead if something as big as you bit me."

There was an air of disappointment from the large beetle-looking thing. "We are them and they are us."

She narrowed her eyes. "Like a hive? All of you? Are you communicating with the krottel in other areas of the ship?"

"We are one who make up a body. The others are one. We are one being, the krottel, but so much of the magic we consume is used to make up the image of a being, we can't speak over great distances as well."

Viera shook her head. "Then why not use a magic soak like the rest of us?"

"It isn't enough. We need pure magic."

Viera's head spun with all the new information. Bugs pretending to be humanoid. Pure magic, impure magic. *What the actual fuck?* "So, after I soaked in the magic in the shower it was pure enough for you?"

"No. we need it from a planet."

A shiver of dread made the food in Viera's belly feel heavy and unwanted. Her voice came out low and shaky. "Only the planet's pure magic works for you?"

"Yes."

"Can you create your own magic on a planet?"

"No."

"Earth still won't work for you."

"Untrue."

"Very true. You saw my memories. Humans will fight." *It's like debating with my second graders. I don't want it to be true, so it's not true, so neener!*

Viera shook her head, and the room spun. Her vision was starting to dim, though she wasn't sure why. Her hands slammed down on the table to keep her from falling.

"Sit, human, your body is adjusting—"

"I don't need any more of your tales. I'm fine. I'm just..." She didn't know what. Lightheaded? She didn't feel well.

"Your body is changing. The bite didn't kill you instantly, but it did kill the person you were. We didn't plan this, but now—"

The door slammed open. Thorn and Flower Prancer stormed in. Thorn's head jerked back and forth as she took in the room quickly and ran towards Viera. "What the hell is this?" She slid an arm around Viera for support.

Flower Prancer's eyes narrowed at the largest of the bugs. "We were planning on staying out of it, krottel, but you've changed the rules. We'll see you at the summit tomorrow morning."

Viera felt swimmy as she nearly passed out, but she distinctly heard Thorn snap, "Krottel? For fuck's sake! This is what's under their robes?"

24

Let's Pretend This Didn't Happen

Viera

For a moment, Viera wondered if she imagined the two in the room. *How can they be here? There were so many openings when we walked the halls. They can't be here.*

Thorn's arm slid around her waist and boosted Viera up. "Lean on me. We have to go."

"Why don't the krottel make scurrying sounds?"

The other woman practically carried her out of the room. "That's your first question?"

A groan of pain escaped her. Her muscles were cramping, but she didn't want to stay on this ship.

Put one foot in front of the other. Isn't there a song from a Christmas cartoon about that? Her mind wandered as her vision blurred.

Thorn's voice snapped her out of her musing. "Viera, we need to hurry."

Next to them, Flower Prancer paused, forcing them to stop. The large unicorn-looking creature with beautiful rainbow hair sniffed her. It started at her toes, then her belly, and ended at Viera's neck. "This will never do. She's drained."

Thorn tugged a bit, bracing Viera more snugly to her side. "What do you suggest, Elder?" There was a level of reverence to her voice, but also an underlayer of annoyance. They were in a hurry and Thorn was doing the best she could.

Viera sighed. "Give me a second. I can walk on my own. The hallway should stop spinning if I just get more oxygen into my poor brain."

"No," snapped Flower Prancer. "Put the human on my back."

As Thorn exclaimed, "What?" Viera felt like cold water had been dumped over her head. She remembered the shock Scout had at the mere suggestion of riding one of these honored creatures.

She couldn't ... wouldn't ... be the one to dishonor a yonat.

Thorn's voice snapped her out of her musing. "You heard me, Commander Firoza. We don't have time to argue."

"It's forbidden."

"No, it's forbidden if we *say* it's forbidden," he said with a sigh.

Thorn started to do as Flower Prancer demanded, though she still argued. "What will the others think? What will they say? Humans are already thought of as savages for not having mastered space."

The yonat's head dropped as he snuffed in a very horse-like sound of disgust. "Let me worry about that."

Viera's voice came out soft. "I can't, it's ... I can't."

The violet eyes of the yonat snapped to her. "Act like your Rainbow Brite and be strong!"

Gob-smacked, Viera's jaw dropped open. She did as she was told.

Once on Flower Prancer's back, they moved faster. The white walls zoomed by ... at least she assumed they did. Again, nothing really seemed to change except the occasional turns.

Viera braced herself, hugging Flower Prancer with her knees and arms, lying low so as not to slow his movements.

When they got to the portal to the space station, two krottel in bipedal form stood blocking their passage. "You will not take the human."

Flower Prancer snorted. "She is not yours to keep."

"We need her," one of them explained. "You can't take her."

"You are stacking up your crimes, krottel. Let us pass." Flower Prancer sounded angry, his head lowered. A low vibration began in his body.

"Not with the human."

Thorn took a step forward, but Flower Prancer said, "No. Meet us at your unit." Then the world shimmered. Viera gaped as everything looked ... she wasn't sure, but it appeared as if they were under water. Then the yonat leapt and they were on the station, racing.

Somehow the creature could run with her on its back and avoid all the other creatures, large and small. Viera just tucked in as small as she could and held on. She tried not to be a burden.

As a child, Viera had dreamed of riding on a unicorn. If she believed the drawings of her students, most young girls did. Flying down the corridors of Torville Station Number Six, the experience wasn't nearly as majestic as she thought it would be. A bit bumpier ... and a lot more terrifying.

When the motion stopped, Flower Prancer grunted, "Off with you. Thorn shouldn't be far behind, but you need to be behind that door. We'll talk tomorrow."

Viera slid down. When she finally took in her surroundings, she realized she stood in front of the unit she, Thorn, and Scout were using. "That was so fast," she whispered in awe.

"In with you, so I can go."

She jerked. The voice came from nowhere. "Were we invisible?"

One of Flower Prancer's annoyed grunts came from her left. "Into the unit, Viera."

She placed her hand on the entrance panel. Once the door slid shut behind her, she trudged to the couch and collapsed.

Can I just sleep here? Never move again?

The pounding of a thousand elephants tensed all her muscles. The ven zoomed past, got to the door, turned and raced towards Scout's room. *God above, Beaver is like a cat. How can a single animal ... one that can fly even, make such a damned ruckus?*

"Ms. Kor! You're back!" Scout ran out and leapt onto her back, giving her a bear hug.

She 'oofed' but reveled in the experience. "Are you okay? Did anyone hurt you?" She knew he'd been fine, but she had to hear it from him.

"I'm okay. I was worried about you."

"I'm here now."

He climbed down. "Are you okay? Do you need to soak?"

Viera groaned. *Do I need a soak?* "I did a double this morning and Flower Prancer said I'd done too much."

"But that was this morning. Are you dizzy? You may need more, Ms. Kor. It's not the same every day."

She thought about it, and in the end, the idea of showering sounded wonderful. "Okay, I'll go shower and soak."

It took way too long to traverse the few steps from the couch to her personal restroom. She stripped off her clothes and stepped into the shower. She'd somewhat gotten used to the showers, but she really wanted to scrub the back of her neck and upper back where the bug had been. Once she was out of the small cleaning cubicle, she wanted to check that area out. *Is there a mark?*

Once she felt quasi-clean, she ran the magical soak. After the first run, her vision sharpened, but her head still felt swimmy. *Damn it, the boy was right.*

She ran it again.

And again.

And again.

Viera stood tall in the shower and took the first steady breath she could remember taking since the super-sweet shake. She massaged her temples and though her head didn't feel fantastic, the pounding had receded to almost nothing. Mentally taking stock of her body in an almost meditative state, she decided she felt ... human.

Outside of the shower, she found Thorn waiting for her. With a wide smile, she gratefully stepped into the other woman's embrace.

25

Yes Ma'am, Can I have Another?

Thorn

Thorn tilted Viera's head up and they kissed. She wrapped her hands around the other woman's hips and pulled her closer, loving the sensation of having someone close.

Their tongues met, and electricity shot to Thorn's core, igniting her like firecrackers. She moaned.

Her hands found the bottom of Viera's tunic, and she slid it up, reveling in the silky, soft skin covering a succulent body. As they kissed, slowly and passionately, she let her hands explore the other woman's luscious body until she reached Viera's plump breasts.

As Viera's thumbs lightly skimmed over Thorn's sensitive abs and back, she trembled and moaned into Viera's mouth. Then she stepped back. "Your bed?"

"Mm-hmm." Viera swayed her hips as she led the way. She gave Thorn a sultry look over her shoulder as Thorn took in every inch of Viera's body. She enjoyed the show as the other woman stripped off her clothes.

When they got to Viera's bed, she spun, smiled at Thorn, and purred, "On the bed, lovely lady."

Thorn made a low sound deep in her throat. She approved of the demand from the smaller human. "Yes, ma'am." She sat and scooted up.

Viera's smile grew as she followed Thorn onto the bed. She began kissing Thorn's leg, nibbling and licking as she traveled up her body.

When she got to Thorn's thigh, she rubbed her hand up, stroking her fingers in more and more enticing ways. She added pressure to all the right spots. She circled the hardening clit, eliciting a whimper as Thorn's body jerked.

She continued to slowly kiss and nibble up Thorn's leg as her finger slid in. Every muscle in Thorn tightened in pleasure as Viera's finger stroked in and out. Thorn's body gyrated up and down as her whimpers shifted to mewls and moans.

Viera reached Thorn's center and licked up from her finger to her clit and let her tongue circle before she clamped down, adding suction to her tongue's flicks. Thorn lost time as she rode the waves of sensation.

As she climaxed, Thorn screamed, bucking up as she murmured out happy, delirious sounds.

When she finally opened her eyes, she saw Viera watching her. Electricity surged through her at the thought of her enjoyment turning another woman on.

Crawling up Thorn's body from foot to treasure box, she trailed her tongue as she went. Viera made sounds of passion as she explored Thorn's body. *If she's getting as much out of this as I am, I can only imagine how much more fun we can have together.*

Viera scraped her teeth over one of Thorn's breasts, and then sucked the tip into her mouth. Thorn groaned, arching her back to follow Viera's mouth as it moved away. She reached to play with Viera breasts, enjoying the soft beauty above her.

Thorn pulled Viera down until their mouths met. She leaned forward and hummed. "Good, now rub your hot sauce all over mine. Are you as wet as I am?"

The woman above her rolled her hips, rubbing their clits together. Her breathing got ragged as they kissed, Thorn practically devouring her. *That's it my beauty, my fire cloud. I want to feel you break. Scream for me.*

Thorn's hand rubbed down her back. *Just a bit longer, and I can give Viera ... everything!* She slid her finger in and out of the woman on top of her, enjoying their deep kissing, her taste, and her moans. Their bodies continued to gyrate, bringing Thorn closer to a second climax.

Shifting, Thorn thrust her fingers a bit deeper, and Viera gasped. She moved faster against Thorn, begging for more. Thorn trailed her tongue down the long neck and began to nibble, biting gently, tasting the salty sweat as she sucked.

Viera screamed. "Oh, god Thorn, yes!" And then, body trembling, she collapsed on Thorn like a delectable blanket.

Feeling there was more, Thorn turned them over, so Viera was on her back. She continued to stroke in and out, let her thumb play with Viera's clit, and kissed the woman deeply. She wanted to taste that scream, feel another orgasm around her fingers, and see it when her world exploded.

And then it did.

26

Good With Her Hands

Viera

The next morning, Viera disentangled herself from Thorn, found an outfit from her closet, and went to shower again. Her head pounded, so she decided to do a single magic soak. When it finished, she heard Thorn's voice from the restroom. "Do another, just in case."

Uncertain because of Flower Prancer's warning the day before, she shrugged and hit the button one more time. Once the light turned off, Viera stepped out. Unlike the night before, the room was empty.

A pang of disappointment stabbed her. *Don't, Viera. You know this won't last. You had some fun;*

that was it. Keep it light or you'll break your own heart.

She checked her reflection. She wasn't sure what it was, but for some reason, she thought she looked different.

She brushed her teeth and smoothed back her hair, once again grateful for how short it was.

When she turned to grab the outfit she'd selected, instead of the burnt umber doublet and black slacks, she found a light gray pair of slacks with a matching suit jacket. A shell tank top was neatly folded near the two pieces on the hanger.

Once Viera put on the official clothing that matched Thorn's daily wear, if not a bit lighter in color, she noticed instead of the light-blue double rings Thorn had at the wrists and collar of her outfit, Viera had a single ring of sage green.

Out in the main area, she found Thorn in the same outfit she'd worn every day. "Good morning, fire cloud."

Warm bubbles of happiness grew in Viera. "Good morning, sunshine."

Thorn looked her up and down. "Nice ... very nice. We'll eat here and then head to the summit. I sent Scout to the promenade to eat. Horax will meet him there."

"Okay, sounds good." Viera bit her lip. "Why am I going to the summit? You and Flower Prancer can tell the beings there what happened, right?"

Thorn shrugged. "I don't question the Elders. But a few things. Don't tell anyone that you rode on his back."

"Of course not, I understand that's not to be discussed."

She blew out a huff of air. "Good. Things have been zooming along rather quickly, I wasn't sure how much you knew about their rules. The other thing: I didn't know the Elders had the magic to turn invisible. He shared a lot with us yesterday. That showed a deep trust. We are not going to make him regret it."

Viera swallowed hard as Thorn finished ordering up breakfast. "No, of course not. I'm honored."

"Good, good. I agree. If the krottel start blabbering, no one will believe them, but if I do, or even you, people may look closer."

The panel whirled behind her, and Viera collected the mugs of coffee. "I never would."

Thorn nodded. "Before we get to the summit, can you tell me what happened? We probably should've talked last night, but it was late. You'll probably be asked to share your story, and I want to be able to support you."

"Oh, yeah. I should've expected that." Viera rubbed her head with one hand. She took a sip of coffee then launched into what she could remember since waking up in the stark white room.

When she finished, Thorn's face was tight. "Those assholes. What right do they have? They just think the whole universe is their fucking buffet." Her eyes widened. "I'm sorry." She shook her head and slid her hands across the table. "I just ... they are so arrogant ... and gross. I had no idea they were bugs!"

A laugh bubbled out of Viera. "That took me by surprise as well. Maybe it's good we got that cleared up. It's taken me a bit to get it sorted out, and I think you need to be desensitized as well."

"Yeah, probably." Thorn stood to get the breakfast plates from the panel. "Anything else you think we should discuss before we get to the meeting?"

Viera sipped her coffee. "If magic can only be created on a planet, how is it produced in the shower? Where does the 'soak' come from?"

Thorn chuckled softly. "You're asking the wrong person. It's more of the imbued technology from the dwarfs. They figured out how to saturate the components on planets we visit. The parts are good for something like a thousand uses or something like that. We just recharge the bits every time we're near a planet. It takes about a day."

"You have to recharge your shower?" Viera laughed. "That's amazing."

They tucked in to eat. It was a warm cereal with nuts and fruit. Halfway through her bowl, Viera looked up and smirked, remembering the night before. "Hot sauce?"

"You want hot sauce?"

"No ... I've never heard someone refer to ... ah ... play time ... as 'hot sauce.'"

"Well, you are very hot, my dear, and down there," her eyes dropped as if she could see through the table and Viera's clothes, "you were wet and saucy. It seemed the perfect description to me."

Viera bit her lips to keep from laughing. "I guess you're not wrong."

She continued to eat. A few more bites in, she gazed into the jewel-green eyes of the other woman. "Can I ask, how can you reach your arms so far? I mean, I know you're taller than me, it's just ... it was fantastic."

Thorn smirked. She held out her hands and Viera watched in fascination as her fingers grew. "I'm a shape shifter, love. I can shift my shape. It makes bed play fun!"

Viera's cheeks heated but could only agree.

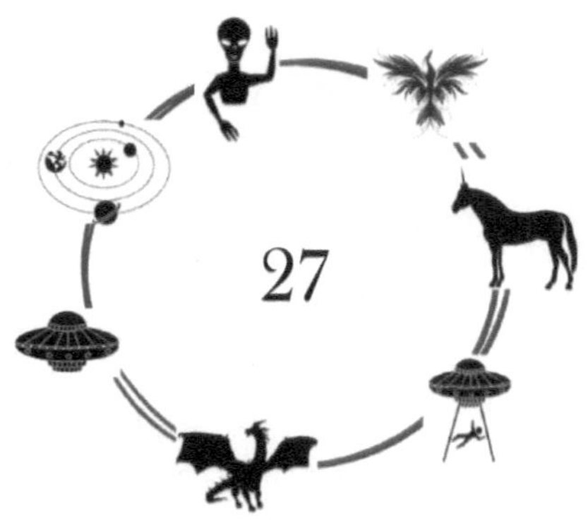

27

Girls Night Out

Betsy

The piles on her desk didn't seem to be getting any smaller. "I swear, I completed that job yesterday and filed everything away. I made the follow-up calls and got everything tidied up. For fuck's sake, I need a secretary ... ha! Like that's ever going to happen." She glared at the pile for good measure, though it didn't seem at all phased.

Betsy shook her head and thought about what it would take to bring someone on as an administrative assistant in her office. *Well, now would be as good a time as any ... I guess.* She'd have to consider it. Next week, there was a group call, and she'd bring it up then.

It was getting late. This evening was her girls' night out with Viera. She'd been shocked that the other woman hadn't spent some part of each day talking her ear off. Viera *had* mentioned wanting a staycation away from all drama. *And I did tell her to get away. Maybe she took my advice and went four hours out of town. That would be ... shocking. That woman doesn't leave the area for anything.*

Betsy chuckled as she finished packing her bag, slipping her phone into a pocket, and heading out. She made sure the office was locked and secured before trudging to her car. She was tired. The week had been particularly long. She had a group of clients, and her main contact was on vacation ... of course she was, and the secondary contact was nervous. Every few hours there was a call with some issue that turned out to be nothing.

There was no telling her client it was nothing; she had to slowly walk the client through each point until the client felt satisfied. It was grueling.

In her car, she slumped. "I could really use a girl's night. I miss Viera. Even if it's a silly movie and homemade margaritas. Anything to forget my week ... and it's only Tuesday!" She huffed out a laugh.

The trip from her office to Viera's place was quick. The city wasn't big and, it being after six, there wasn't much traffic. She used the time to shift from the work headspace to the friend headspace.

When she arrived at Viera's house, all the lights were out. And Viera's car was gone.

Huh? Maybe she forgot something and just headed to the store.

Betsy parked and got out of her car. She walked around Viera's house. It felt ... cold ... empty. She went back to the mailbox. It was stuffed full. There is a *lot* of mail here. She took the contents and headed back to the house, her gut starting to churn. *This isn't good.*

At the back door, she used a lockpicking trick her dad had taught her to get the door open. The back door led into a small kitchen. It was big enough for a small breakfast nook with two chairs, all the basic appliances, and almost no counter space.

She tossed the mail onto a counter. "Hello? Viera? It's me, Betsy. You're not answering ... well, anything."

Betsy turned on a light and looked around. A coffee mug and plate sat in the sink. Nothing else. *Did you have lunch out today? Did you even eat here today? Are those the dishes from a different day?*

The kitchen led into a living room, a larger, less cramped space, with an oversized couch, two large chairs, a coffee table, and a huge TV. The couch didn't have a blanket on it, no dishes on the coffee table, nothing. The room was spotless. Her gut tightened. This wasn't right ... not at all. The place was too tidy for a staycation.

Betsy headed up the stairs, continuing to call out, and checked the bedrooms and bathroom. Nothing looked like it had been touched in hours ... many hours.

Not liking the lonesome feel she got from the house, Betsy left through the back door, turning off the lights and locking up. "The last place I spoke to Viera was the school ... there's no way."

She drove to the elementary school. There was one car in the parking lot ... Viera's. It was time to use her private detective skills. Her friend was obviously missing.

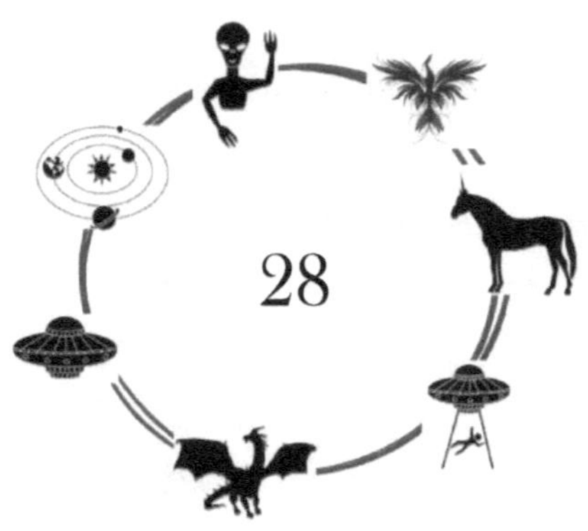

Chapter 28 - Always The Last To Know

Viera

Thorn and Viera took the lift to a locked floor. A code had to been typed in to reach the level. When they disembarked, there weren't many beings around. Thorn led her to a large room.

A huge, arched entrance opened to an arena with tiers.

Viera paused at the top of the wide-open space and her eyes immediately found the krottel sitting at a table at the center. A cold wave of terror washed through her. She gulped. *They can't hurt you here.*

There are tons of ... beings. You are safe. The Elders are here, Thorn is by your side, don't be a ninny.

Thorn placed a hand on the small of her back. She leaned down and whispered in her ear, "Don't worry, I'm here. You're not alone."

With a shaky breath, Viera looked around. Each tier of the space had a grouping of chairs, pillows, and tables for the creatures to meet with their committees. Most of the arena was empty, but scattered throughout were representatives of the different aliens Viera had seen during her stay at Torville Station Number Six.

A large ramp went from the entrance to the center. Thorn walked with confidence past five levels to the ground floor. The bottom of the arena seemed to stretch the length of a football field. There were three tables set up in the center of the circular room. Flower Prancer stood by another yonat. A second table, of course, had three of the krottel standing behind it. Thorn led them to the last table. Another of her people already stood by the table. A tall man with wavy purple hair. His outfit matched Thorns down to the double, colored stripes, though his were purple. She wondered what the different colors meant.

I'll have to ask her about that later ... if there's time. Maybe Scout knows.

At the table, the two tapped fists above where humans had hearts and bowed their heads. The man said, "Commander."

Thorn replied with, "Major." She then turned to Viera. "Major Shifts, this is Viera Kor, the Earthling that went missing. Flower Prancer requested she join us today."

Major Shifts repeated the greeting to Viera. She placed her fist on her heart and dipped her head. "Major Shifts, it's an honor to meet you."

There weren't any seats on the stage, unlike the viewing tiers, so they all turned to face the yonat.

Flower Prancer's tail swished. "We are here to announce our final verdict on the claim the chanzii brought up that the krottel are invading planets, destroying them, and moving on, without care for the beings living on the planets. They request from this council and the Elders that sanctions be placed on the invasive colonization force before they destroy more planets."

The room grew still. Flower Prancer moved from behind his table and gazed at the different beings in the room. "I left yesterday with a plan for today's message. I come today with different thoughts. I met with my delegation last night, and we spoke long into the wee hours. Before I give our final verdict, I feel obligated to impart more information to the room at large."

An impending sense of doom overcame Viera. Part of her guessed that was why she'd been asked to come, but the idea of her story being shared with all these people made her feel a bit sick.

The yonat's restless pacing around the room ended in front of her. "Viera, can you tell the group what happened yesterday?"

She swallowed, her mouth suddenly dry. A shiver ran down her back as she remembered the sensation of the bug on her skin. Her hands shook so she stuffed them in her pockets. She licked her lips. "I, um ... yeah. I can do that." Though she spoke softly, her words seemed to reverberate throughout the room. It seemed every creature's attention shifted to her.

"I object." One of the krottel at the other table lifted its hand, one finger raised.

The yonat still behind the table swished its tail. "You'll have your turn, krottel. The human will speak now."

Thorn placed a hand on Viera's shoulder and spoke softly into her ear. "It's okay. This is a sealed meeting. Nothing spoken here leaves the room. Just breathe and do your best."

Viera nodded her understanding. "I was in the promenade." She briefly wondered if the word she'd been using for that giant area was universal. Then she wondered if it mattered. She shook her head. She had to focus, not spiral. "My companion went to get us water to drink when I felt a pain on the back of my head ..."

She went on to explain what happened. When she tried to skip over details, either Flower Prancer, his companion, Thorn, or Major Shifts would ask questions.

Despite not interrupting her again, Viera could sense the krottel's agitation at the situation. Some of the opinions she added, like her confusion at how far they took her to get to the restroom, clearly caused the three krottel angst.

Afraid the community at large will learn your dirty little secret, are you? Well, maybe kidnapping humans is a bad pastime, bucko!

"Then I felt a sharp pain on the back of my neck, and I remembered the threat that the bug would cause instant death. I thought about my family, but also young Scout and how he'd feel. I imagined how sad all my students would be back home. It was too much. I was suddenly overwhelmed with all my emotions. I yelled 'no!'" She bit her lip. It occurred to her how dumb that sounded. "I don't know why. It isn't like you can yell at a bug bite and make death stop."

Flower Prancer's cool violet gaze met hers. "Apparently, you can, human."

She looked down at her hands, still attached to her very alive body and gave the yonat a small smile. "I guess. But I don't understand how."

He backed up a few paces and faced the crowd. "I'd like to tell my tale. Yesterday, after the meeting, I had made up my mind. As you all know, we Elders are very interested in letting each race experience their own course of evolution without interference. We do *not* approve of changing the natural run of a species. Even when that means one creature invades another's world."

He moved around the stage, letting his words sink in. "This case brought in a new level of complication because worlds are being drained of their magic. If this were to continue, solar systems and galaxies could start to degrade. This larger question needs to be discussed within the panel of five on the yonat home world. It is not for this council."

Again, Viera could feel the weight of his words. She felt like a toddler at the grown-ups' table. She knew why she'd been invited, but it still felt wrong.

Next to her, she saw Thorn's normally glowing complexion dim with her fear. The reality of what was coming terrified her as much as it worried Viera. It felt like the weight of multiple worlds sat on their shoulders.

God, I just want to be back in my classroom teaching the kiddos. Why can't my biggest worry be a skinned knee? Then again, I'm glad Thorn isn't alone. I'm glad I can be here for her. God, I can't even make up my mind.

Finally, Flower Prancer turned back, and his gaze bored into her. "But back to my story.

Commander Thorn Firoza approached me because her companion, an Earth woman, had disappeared. The woman had been playing a game with her son, and when Scout had gone to get a drink, he'd returned to find her missing."

He shifted to face the crowd and Viera felt like a cord between them had been cut. He faced the krottel. "As some of you know, and others do not, I can smell magic. I'd sniffed the woman earlier that morning and knew her scent. I followed it to the krottel ship. It was faint. We searched, but the ship is a maze, and we'd lost time."

Viera could feel something coming. The yonat buzzed with ... something. His eyes glowed as he faced first his companion and then the crowd at large. "And then it hit me, the smell, the feel, the taste. A blast of pure energy—a star, a flame, an emergence—that flared to life. The beginning." Flower Prancer turned and took two steps towards the bug people. "The krottel awoke the wizard within the human. All unknowing, they created a sixth pillar for Earth."

29

A Pillar Of Society

Viera

Viera swayed on her feet. Arms wrapped around her, stopping her from collapsing on the floor. For a moment she debated passing out and escaping the remainder of the summit, but she knew that wasn't going to happen.

Pillar? I'm a fucking pillar? A wizard? ... I can do ... magic?

She started breathing fast, her heart pounding like a snare drum in her chest. Thorn's arms squeezed her tighter. "Just breathe, Viera. We'll figure this out."

"Right. Breathe. Just that easy."

Her warm breath tickled Viera's ear as she laughed softly. "Exactly. Just that easy."

"Did you know?"

"No. I didn't."

While they spoke, the room erupted in talk and argument. When she looked up, Viera saw the audience staring at her, she looked down at her feet and tried to ignore that she was on a stage.

Finally, Flower Prancer made a loud neighing sound, magically enhanced, and everyone quieted. "To continue. The power that the Earth woman expended was enough for me and Commander Thorn Firoza to follow. We found her. The krottel tried to stop us from taking her back. They wanted to keep her. I have my suspicions, but now that you know the human's story and my story, we will allow the krottel to speak."

There was a moment of silence, then a tension in the room. Viera could feel it as the attention of the beings in the arena shifted to the three bug-people at the other table.

Is this sense something I've always had, or part of the stupid magic they opened up in me? Wait. Not stupid. I can fucking do magic! That isn't stupid, that's fantastic! They're stupid. What they did to me was horrible, and scary, but ... oh, my God, magic!

She knew her mind was reeling, and she needed to get a hold of herself. She could freak out later.

"You had no right to enter our ship, yonat."

All around the tiers, there were sounds of astonishment from the different creatures. The sounds came out different, from gasps, to snorts, to ruffled feathers, to stomped hooves. But the message was clear: No one speaks to an Elder like this.

The vibration that Viera felt coming from Flower Prancer earlier intensified. He gazed at the spokes-bug ... Viera didn't know how to think of the krottel. "You have committed crimes, krottel. If I were to exact punishment here and now, your secrets would come out, and no amount of *quiet* would keep those secrets from becoming common knowledge. If you dare to make another baseless accusation, I will happily show you the consequence of denying me exit from your ship yesterday evening. I know it was your companion who stopped me. And if you dare question me one more time, I *will* drink up the magic you currently have. Do you understand?"

"Yes, Elder."

The krottel's voice didn't change. It didn't sound sorry or scared or even cowed by the threat. It just agreed in a monotone voice.

Flower Prancer stared at it for another moment before saying, "Do you want to state your side of the story?"

"We will die without magic."

"False," the yonat said. "You can give us truths in this summit—you know the rules. I will not tolerate lies."

The krottel glided around the table and Viera tensed. Thorn had moved away once Viera had regained her balance and now Viera stepped closer to her. Her attention was on the krottel, but a warmth filled her as Thorn clasped her hand in solidarity.

"We need magic to survive, just like all of you. But unlike you, we can't produce it. We are looking for a planet that will sustain us. We heard you and the qynad tell the human her world is rich in magic. As you said before, you are not the guardians, the watchers, the peacekeepers, of the galaxy. If we can find Earth, the magic is ours to aid in our survival. We don't want to die off."

Fear ran down her spine. The creature sounded so reasonable, but it was her planet, her people, that it spoke of so cavalierly. She wanted to argue, even knowing it wouldn't help.

Flower Prancer's tail swished. "You changed the rules when you took the human. That was a first strike. Your third strike was blocking me from leaving your ship. But the second strike, and let me make this clear, the reason we were planning to step back after the second day of the summit is because we as the Elders are against getting in the way of an alien race's natural evolution."

Flower Prancer's companion, a dark gray yonat with a mane and tail in shades of blues and purples, walked over to the krottel standing at the end of the table. He touched his gold horn past the mask and a pulse of power flashed through the room. The cape and mask crumpled to the ground.

The spokes-being for the krottel yowled. After the screeching sound—reminiscent of nails on a chalkboard—ended, it turned to the darker yonat. "Why?"

The other yonat voice came out like a song, though his words were a snarl. "We told you your companion would be punished for blocking an

Elder's way. The question wasn't if, but how. Your secret has been kept, krottel, be thankful, not argumentative, or we will seek out the other guard for punishment."

"You will not visit Earth, krottel, nor will any of the rest of your race. You will leave the chanziian planet. There are plenty of planets that are uninhabited. We are placing sanctions. You will not invade inhabited planets. You are not trustworthy. The people of Earth do not know about space travel, other beings, or magic. If you invade, you will upset their natural growth. You have no care for them as a species, as was proven with what you did with Viera, their representative."

The krottel pointed at Thorn. "Will you punish her for showing the human this space station, other beings, and the potential of magic?" It shifted to point at a qynad. "Will you punish this beast, who told the Earthling about magic and tainted her with more knowledge?" It dropped its arm and rotated to Flower Prancer. "Or are my people the only ones getting punished this day, Elder?"

The gray yonat stepped forward. "Commander Thorn Firoza introduced one human to space travel. If we thought that would infect the species, yes, we would sanction her and her race. But we can read the human's intentions; she will not spread the tale. After invading her memories, you know that as well as we do. As for Horax telling her about magic, it was the only way to keep her healthy once she'd left Earth. Again, it is a single case. There have been other single case Earthlings who have known, but none have *ever* made them a wizard, forced the evolution—none before you. That is *your* crime."

With a glow to his eyes, he stepped towards the krottel. "And none of the beings you have mentioned have let Earth as a whole know about intelligent life elsewhere. You threaten them with your invasion. As Flower Prancer said, we have placed sanctions on you. Leave all inhabited planets you now occupy. Do *not* invade any others. Do you understand?"

There was a tense silence, and then the creature said, "Yes, Elder. We understand."

30

But Can I Use My Phone With Magic?

Viera

Viera stood next to Thorn on the lift back up to the rooms they shared. Her body trembled as she realized how calm everything felt. It was like the buzz of everyone around her suddenly was turned off.

What the hell are you thinking, Viera? You're just shook up from learning about what the awful bug-people did.

"Can you believe it? We won!" Thorn looked awed. "I hoped. I went in telling myself we could do it, but deep in my gut, I didn't think it would work. The Elders ... you know the Ents were modeled after them. Immovable trees. They move slowly and take forever to make a decision."

"Until they don't," Viera mumbled.

When they got to the room, Thorn leaned down to kiss Viera's forehead. "Go on. It's G-fourteen. We'll pack, eat, then be on our way. My son needs to acclimate to Earth time and gravity before heading back to school."

Viera rubbed her forehead. Everything felt off, but it was different than when she'd left Earth. She wasn't sure why. She faced Scout's room a moment before his door swung open. His eyes were bright, smile wide, and he sounded as hopeful as excited. "Did we win? Can we go home?"

Thorn squatted to be face to face with her son. "We did win, but it'll take some time for the krottel to leave and our people to return. It may be an Earth year or two before we make it back home."

Scout's face showed all his emotions. He jerked up with a start of a cheer when he'd heard they won, but then he fell with a droop at the time it would take for them to get home. Thorn wrapped him in a hug.

She kissed each of his cheeks. "Go pack your things, sweetness. We're heading back to Earth.

We have other news to share. I think things are about to get—" she gazed up at Viera, "—interesting."

Viera could feel the love between mother and son as they hugged in front of her. It made her think of the people back on Earth she'd abandoned for the last few days. *What must they think? Would any of them be worried? Would my parents even notice?*

As soon as she had that thought, she knew it was unworthy. Betsy was probably frantic. How had she not thought about Betsy until now? Her life was going to be a mess when she got home.

She rubbed the back of her neck. "Do you know the day and time back on Earth? My phone and watch died."

Thorn stood and looked at her, as if confused. "Why didn't you charge them?"

"I could charge them?" Everything about that statement seemed anathema. She stood on an alien space station with all sorts of advanced technology alongside the magic. Of course they'd have a charge cord for her phone. Why wouldn't they?

"We'll get your things charging once we get back on the Ziner."

"Um. Okay, but ... Earth?"

"Oh, right." She tapped the watch on her wrist. "At G-fifteen, it'll be two a.m. on Wednesday morning back in Wisconsin. We'll start to readjust to Earth time once we're on the ship. Now, go get your things packed." She checked her watch again. "Can you be ready in a half-hour? Maybe an hour?"

"Ah ... sure." Viera's mine whirled with so much information. *Wednesday? I missed girls' night out? How will I ever explain this to Betsy? Fuck! She's going to send every government agency out to find me. This is going to be bad ...*

Thorn spun and disappeared into her room. Scout ran into his room. "Off my bed, you lazy ven!"

Beaver ran out, coming to Viera's feet with wide eyes, begging for attention. Viera could almost feel the beast's hope. She knelt on the floor and petted the excited, soft creature. She needed the comfort as much as the beastie did.

Why would I even need thirty minutes? I didn't bring anything with me. I have my phone and watch. I think I can collect those things in about a minute.

Scout stuck his head out. "Don't you need to pack?"

With a laugh she shook her head. "What would I pack, silly? I have my phone and watch. That's pretty much all I had on me when we left the classroom."

He shrugged and went back into his room to get his stuff gathered.

Viera stood and walked into the room she'd used as hers for two days. She changed from the suit she'd worn to the summit into the jeans and shirt she'd been wearing when she'd been beamed up. *Beam me up ... Horax!* On a side table, she found her watch and phone; the first she clipped to her wrist, the second fit into her pocket.

In the closet were all the clothes she'd worn. *I wonder where they got these clothes and what happens to them now? Do they have a second-hand store for stowaways? 'Come dress your stowaway so they don't run away naked!'* She snorted as she shut the doors.

She walked back out and sat on the couch. Her mind zoned out as she lounged. Time became unreal ... like most of the week. Eventually, Thorn came out with her bag and sat down next to her. "What's on your mind?"

"Will I be able to use my phone if I am now a pillar? A wizard?"

Thorn's eyebrows came together with her confusion. "I don't understand."

"I don't know, I've read books where magic and technology don't mix. Others where they do. I just ... what do I believe?"

"Viera, we've done little but talk about the thick blanket of magic that covers your world. If magic and technology couldn't co-exist, how could your world have any form of phones or computers, planes or cars, smart watches, or the internet?"

Viera's head dropped as she laughed. *I do not sound hysterical.* "Okay, yeah. That makes sense."

"I wanted to ask. I know we're just doing something 'light' ... but I don't know what 'light' means to a human."

Fear and hope slammed into Viera. Her emotions seemed more powerful then she thought they should be, but everything seemed so intense. "Okay."

"Do you want to share my room on the Ziner?"

"Oh, yeah. That sounds really good." Viera leaned over to give Thorn a kiss. "I'd like that."

Before they could discuss anything else, there was a knock on the door. Beaver dashed to the entrance, launching at the last moment and attacking the entry with two feet up.

Scout followed his pet from his room. "I'll get it! I'll get it!" The second time he said it, it was more insistent, as if someone had argued with him. In reality, neither Viera nor Thorn had moved.

At the door, he checked the window panel to make sure it wasn't anyone unsafe, then swung the door wide.

Flower Prancer walked in, head held high, gazing down at them. "Commander Thorn Firoza. Human Viera Kor. I have decided to join you on your sojourn to Earth."

31

Best Son In The Galaxy

Thorn

Thorn circled her room, checking that she'd packed all her items. Excitement thrummed through her to finally be leaving the space station and heading to a planet. She missed the sun, and real gravity, and space to move around.

Leaving Torville Station Number Six meant stripping the room. *Scout and I will have to make sure to double check Viera's room. She won't know that everything in the unit is ours.*

Once her bags were all packed, she brought them into the main room. There was a platform the ship's crew could transmit the bags from so they didn't have to lug everything through the crowded corridors. It had taken special permission from the station's commandant to allow for this, but they were leaving a bit early, and the halls would be teaming with creatures.

Next she needed to check on Scout. He was good at packing ... as good as any kid. Thorn knocked on his door. "Hey, Scout, it's Mom. Can I come in?"

"Sure, come in. I'm not doing much." *That doesn't sound good.* He lay on his bed, playing on a tablet. Beaver slept on a ven bed, on her back, her paws in the air, mimicking running. *Cute girl is imagining running in the fields. She loves to fly, but she also desires to run and play. We need to get her off this station. I hope she found friends to bond with while we were here.*

"It doesn't look like you've packed. Do you need help?"

He sat up. "My clothes are mostly done."

"Is something wrong, sweetie? You seem glum. We're going home. Aren't you excited?" She gave him a smile, trying to get him to smile back.

His face scrunched up. "We're *not* going home, we're going back to Earth. And because of me and my mess-up, Ms. Kor almost *didn't* get to go home." He covered his face and curled into a ball.

"Oh!" Thorn gathered her son in her arms. "I'm so sorry you've been feeling these big emotions." She rocked Scout. "First of all, do not blame yourself for what the krottel did to your teacher—that is one hundred percent on them. They wanted to capture Viera ... Ms. Kor ... and nothing you did was going to stop them."

Scout sniffled on her lap. She squeezed him tighter. Beaver leapt onto the bed to cuddle into them.

"I'm just glad they didn't hurt you to get to her. I'm sure Viera would agree. When she told me her story, her biggest fear when she originally realized she'd been abducted was that you were taken too. So please, sweetie, just breathe, and don't burden yourself with this." She rubbed his back, trying to soothe him.

"But ... I was supposed to watch her."

"No, Scout. You and she were supposed to entertain each other. We are on the Torville Station Number Six. The Elders are here. No one should've been in any danger. And the krottel paid for their hubris."

He leaned back and gazed at her. "By having sanctions placed on them?"

"Amongst other things, yes."

He smiled wanly. "I just ... I'm so sorry that they kidnapped her."

"I am, too, sweetums. I am, too." She squeezed him again. "Now, let's pack up this room of yours. Then we can head to the ship."

"What about Ms. Kor's room?" He bit his lip and sounded nervous.

"We'll do that later. I want to walk, stretch my legs, don't you? And," she tapped his nose, "I'm hungry. We can eat on the ship, then come back and see what she's packed and what she left for us."

A smile took over his face. "Just us? I've missed spending time with you, Mom."

She kissed his forehead. "I missed 'us' time too, sweetie. I promise, just us."

32

Aren't I The Teacher?

Viera

Viera sat on the bed of the room she now shared with Thorn. A small thrill buzzed through her that she'd have all the extra time with Thorn. She knew getting addicted to the alien woman was an awful idea, but they hadn't had nearly enough time to play ... especially once she learned about shapeshifting fingers.

Her face heated at the naughty thought.

Scout knocked on the edge of the door. "Hi, Ms. Kor. I've brought your bag."

"My bag? I don't have a bag."

"Sure you did. You didn't pack it, but when Mom went in and saw that, she and I packed for you."

Her head spun. "I don't have anything out here. All I brought were the clothes on my back, and my phone. What did you two pack?"

He dragged a bag over to the bed and then laboriously hefted it up. When Viera made to help, he shook his head. "I got it." Once fully on the bed he beamed at her. "Yes!"

She scooted over and unzipped the bag. Inside were all the clothes from the closet. In a side pocket were the toiletries from the restroom, as well as towels. "You took everything?"

"Each species brings everything into the rooms. We even took the bedding, but Mom packed that into a storage area. That's what we'd gone into your room for, the bedding. She didn't realize you didn't know to get the rest of it ... now you do!"

Viera had so many things she wanted to say, but not to Scout. Instead she just asked, "Do you know how I can get my watch and phone charging?" She kept making silly assumptions; she had to just ask all the questions of anyone in front of her.

"Of course!" He took her items and placed them in a cubby. "They'll be ready in about ... um ... an Earth hour."

Gah! How often does this kid have to translate on the fly to accommodate me? "Thank you, Scout."

He smiled before scampering away.

Okay, Viera, no more funk! She pushed herself from the bed and moved the bag to a small table next to the wall. She debated hanging up the clothes ... her clothes ... but wasn't sure it was worth it for two days.

Thorn was off getting the ship prepared for separation from the station so they could head back to Earth. She suggested everyone try to sleep. It was time to acclimate to Earth time, and they'd eat later. So that was the plan. The problem was, Viera was too hyped up.

Well, she'd never fall asleep if all she was doing was pacing the room. If she could get a few minutes sleep now, maybe she could avoid the worst of the jet-lag later ... ha!

A warm kiss woke her. Reaching up, Viera twined her fingers through Thorn's hair, which cascaded around her in a waterfall of purple. She deepened the kiss, decided this may be the best way to wake up she'd ever experienced. The alarm clock industry could go out of business with this discovery.

Thorn pulled back. "I don't know about you, but I'm hungry. Wanna get some food?"

Viera pushed up from the bed, thinking food was the last thing on her mind. "What time is it? I really need to at least learn your numbers. Why doesn't your silly learning program start with that? Numbers and coffee?"

After giving her another quick kiss, Thorn dragged Viera from the bed. "Most young kids don't care about what time it is, that's why. It's equivalent to noon, Wednesday, central standard time on Earth."

"Oh!" Viera said brilliantly. "We're switching?"

"It'll help us all adjust."

Viera rubbed her face before getting out of bed. "Should I change?"

"Sure. We have time for you to change, maybe even go to the restroom if you'd like. I'll wait."

She went to her bag and found a pair of black linen pants and a cerulean doublet. She couldn't find a belt and grunted.

"What's wrong?"

"I can't find a belt."

"If you'd hung up your clothes, it would've been easier. Go, use the toilet, I'll find you something." Thorn waved her off with a shooing motion.

Once she was in clean clothes, she washed her face and finger-brushed her hair. *Stupid toiletries, all in my stupid unpacked bag, in the stupid other room.* Thorn's voice came back to her ... modified. *"If you'd unpacked, it would've been easier."* Poppycock! *Okay, maybe she's not completely wrong.*

Viera walked out, dressed, though her top was more like a blousy dress. Viera held out a thick black belt. She secured it, and they headed out.

Looking down at her outfit, Viera asked, "Do the colors of my outfit mean anything?"

"Not with your skin tone."

"Wait, what?" Viera's arms shot out as she searched the top's color for some meaning.

"I'm joking. It only has meaning in the official outfits we wore to the summit. This is just the basic outfit of our citizens. Like humans, there used to be a vast variety of fashion on our world, but without a world, we don't have any way to express ourselves."

When they arrived at the mess hall, they sat at a table already occupied by Scout. Viera gazed around and realized she started to recognize some of the other beings. "How did Horax do in his competitions?"

Scout beamed. "He made it to the third round. He's invited back for the next series."

Thorn tapped on the table then signaled to Scout. He scamped off. "He'll go get what I ordered for lunch."

"When we get to Earth, will the beasts that don't blend take the ship and leave?"

"Some will stay on the ship in orbit. The ship can stay hidden pretty easily. Others will beam down to uninhabited areas. We have a settlement on an island. It allows them to stretch their legs."

Viera wondered how much her head could take. "How many Earthlings know about all of this?"

"There are the five pillars, six if we include you. All six know." Thorn smiled. "Most of the major governments have someone in them who knows. We've tried to be good neighbors."

"This is why humans think there are conspiracies ... there *are* conspiracies!"

Scout returned with meatloaf and mac and cheese.

Before they could continue, Flower Prancer came over to their table. "Afternoon, Viera. I hope you are doing well."

"I am, thank you."

"Good, good. Then we can start your training after this meal?"

Abracadabra

Viera

"My what now?" A piece of macaroni fell from Viera's fork as she gaped at the yonat. *Did Flower Prancer decide to join us because of me?*

"Finish eating, human. From what I understand, magic takes extra energy. For most wizards, they're born using magic, they know what their body needs, but you'll have a learning curve with this as well. So, you'll need to eat more than you're used to eating. Then come to the training room in an hour." He bobbed his head and walked off.

"My what now?" Viera asked again to the space Flower Prancer had stood.

Thorn rubbed her back. "Finish that bite and we'll figure this out."

She did, and the cheesy flavor soothed her Wisconsin heart. She took another bite and moaned at how good it tasted. Once she'd had a session of cheese therapy, she leaned back. "I'm getting magic lessons?"

Across the table, Scout giggled. "You're not a student, you're the teacher!"

"That's right, kiddo! But we're always learning ... lifelong learners! I guess in magic, I'm a beginner. Like, even below that, really."

Thorn sipped her mug of tea. "After telling us he'd be joining us, he only showed up again to get his room assignment. There was never a discussion about his goal for joining our venture. Are you okay with this?"

Viera picked up her mug and was happy to see coffee. "I need to learn, right?"

"Yes."

"And the sooner I start ... the better? I mean, I'm not getting any younger, right?"

Thorn sighed into her mug. "True. But waiting a day or two days wouldn't make that much of a difference."

"True, but what else can I do during the trip? I don't understand anything on the ship."

Thorn leaned over to give her a quick kiss. "And I'm too busy for other diversions."

"Gross, Mom!"

She laughed. "Okay. Scout can show you where to go at the right time."

Once they'd figured out her magic lesson ... *Magic lessons! Betsy will never believe this! Wait, I can't tell Betsy, for fuck's sake. Damn it!*

They finished their meal. Thorn had to get back to the main deck of the ship. In the few hours that Viera had slept, they'd left the station far behind. They were trying to make good time to the GPS.

"We're a bit early, Ms. Kor. Do you want me to show you the training room, or take you back up to your room?" Scout was looking around like he had somewhere to be.

"Do you have plans?" There was a slight nervousness from the boy. Viera couldn't quite put her finger on it, but she knew it was something.

"Oh, it's nothing. I'm going to go watch the practice. Horax and a few others. I just don't want to miss anything." He bounced in place.

"Well, then, take me to my trainer."

His smile grew as he grabbed her hand and pulled her through the mess hall. Beaver, who Viera hadn't noticed sleeping under the table, immediately followed, flying above their heads.

The training rooms were on a lower level.

Viera entered the mostly barren room. There was a table in the center with a pencil on it and a single chair. It didn't surprise her to see Flower Prancer waiting for her. Behind her, the door swung closed. "Welcome, Viera. There are a lot of lessons for you to learn in magic. Because there are only five pillars on Earth, I wanted to ensure you had a trainer right away. I'll be your teacher until I've determined your education is acceptable."

Thinking about it, the idea that one of the five pillars lived near Madison, Wisconsin seemed utterly ludicrous. There was no way.

"Okay, thank you." She meant it. The idea of being trained hadn't even occurred to her. The oversight now seemed strange ... of course she needed to be taught. Magic was probably huge.

"Sit at the table." She did as directed. "Now, I want you to sit on your hands, then move the pencil without physically touching it."

Viera wanted to roll her eyes. *Right, and how am I supposed to do that? Any direction, oh wonderful teacher?* She stuffed her hands under her legs and sighed. She glared at the pencil. She was not surprised when the object didn't move. Leaning forward, she squinted, thinking all sorts of mean and nasty thoughts ... at the pencil. Mocking her, it didn't even scream in terror.

Across the room, she could tell Flower Prancer was no more impressed with her use of magic than the pencil.

"Just imagine what you want the pencil to do, Viera. Any magic you can perform on the object, I'll be able to detect. My sensitivity to magic and its nuances is extraordinary."

Eyes closed, Viera imagined what it meant to be ... well ... a pencil. It started off a yellow utensil with graphite. When it was overused, it had to be sharpened. If another object tapped it, it rolled. What could tap it? A finger? Air? A book? Another pencil?

She opened her eyes. Nothing on the table had changed.

The intensity of Flower Prancer's irritation had. *Does he think I'm not trying?*

Her head started to pound, and she slumped. "Maybe you're wrong. Maybe the krottel didn't make me into a new pillar. Maybe it was all a fluke."

"No, Viera, I can smell the magic on you. And I am never wrong!" His tail swished with his annoyance. "Are you even trying?" He snuffled. "There are a few different ways you should be able to move that pencil, it is why we start with moving an object that rolls. It's simple. Having an affinity to liquid isn't as common, but I should've had a glass of water here as well. It's our first day, and we can't make any assumptions, but for now, we'll stop focusing on gas and solid as your elemental magic proficiency."

Viera had been focusing and pushing. She didn't know what, but she felt drained. Now the yonat spoke about things she could only piece together because she read a lot of books. The idea that they pertained to the real world made her head spin.

"So, wait. Everyone has an elemental magic proficiency?"

"Yes, and one non-elemental one. Magical beings, like the chanzii, have one that allows them to shape shift, the non-elemental proficiency of life magic. If, like you, they are also a wizard, they will gain an elemental proficiency and possibly a different non-elemental one. Wizards, like you, always have two. To be able to train you, we need to determine what they are."

Her stomach clenched. "Is there a book I can read? Will I accidentally turn something to dust, like you did that krottel creature?"

"No, that took a combination of three. Being an Elder, I naturally have more. You will have two that are part of your magical being. You can learn to tap into others, to use them, but not master them like magic users who innately have the proficiency."

Viera shook her head. "I think this is going too fast. I need magic for dummies."

"You are not without intelligence. I've observed you."

She laughed. "Thank you. I just mean a book that breaks it down."

"I will break it down for you. I am your teacher."

But will you do it in a manner that will help me?

With a sigh, Viera looked at the pencil. "I don't know if I can move that."

"I don't know either, but I think we're done for the day." The yonat's body twitched and Viera knew he wasn't pleased with the outcome of the day. She just wasn't sure what more she could've done. His idea of teaching wasn't anything she would define as useful.

Viera stayed behind after Flower Prancer left. She paced the room, wondering what she was supposed to feel that she hadn't. When she was sure the yonat was gone, she flicked the pencil with her fingers, causing it to fly across the table and roll across the floor. She smiled in triumph. "I made it move."

She wiggled her eyebrows in her own success. Then she noticed some graphite dust and wiped it away. "Damn, it was a newly sharpened pencil."

Shaking her head, she lumbered over to pick it up and put it back where it'd been. She didn't think Flower Prancer would be amused at finding it on the floor. Then she left.

If everything went according to plan, maybe she'd find some magic tonight after all.

She smiled as she sauntered out of the room.

34

Portal ... Of A Good Time

Viera

Viera had unpacked her bag, taken a shower, including soaking in magic, then examined her clothing options. Intermixed in the linen pants and doublets were two dresses. *I don't know who did all the shopping for my trip, but they're hired!*

She'd pulled on a dark purple A-line dress with three-quarter length sleeves. It had a lighter purple belt that tied just under her chest and the skirt ended mid-thigh.

She'd spent some time thinking about the stupid pencil, but nothing she tried to move in the room would move without the help of one of her two hands ... or her hip ... or her feet. She was good at kicking things.

The door clicked and Thorn walked in, looking tired. Whereas Viera had gotten a nap, Thorn had been running for hours. "Hey, do you wanna just crash?"

Thorn's gaze raked over her, and she hummed appreciatively. "You found one of the dresses. It looks good on you."

"I'm guessing it'll look good on the floor, and we can try again tomorrow."

The green of Thorn's eyes flared. "Oh, I think we'll be practicing for many nights to get everything perfect. I agree, let's get that number on the floor, and you on the bed." She stalked forward like a predator scenting prey.

Excited, and a bit nervous, Viera took a step back. When Thorn reached her, she gently traced her hands around her with feather-light fingers, examining Viera's body. Chills of anticipation raced down her arms. Enclosed in Thorn's embrace, she heard the slow metallic sound of the zipper opening and Thorn's nails lightly trailing down her back.

She shivered, rubbing her now sensitive chest against the other woman at the slow pleasurable torture.

When she gazed up at Thorn, the other woman captured her mouth in a demanding kiss. Thorn's hands traced back up her back and down her arms. Between the hot mouth and cool electricity from the light fingers trailing over her body, Viera's senses were on overdrive.

She rubbed against Thorn, moaning into her mouth, needing more.

Breaking the kiss and stepping away from her, Viera realized she was suddenly naked. Thorn smiled triumphantly, then slowly stripped off her own clothes, piece by piece. Viera wanted to lick each inch of exposed turquoise skin.

Viera reached out, letting her hand explore the curves and planes of the perfect body before her. Thorn wrapped one hand around her, bringing her closer, her other dropping low.

They both dipped their hands into each other's treasure boxes. Viera slowly circled Thorn's clit, using her obvious enjoyment to help slick the process. Her other hand mirrored the circular motion on one of Thorn's breasts.

Thorn, with her literal magical hand, both stimulated Viera's clit, and pushed a finger in and out of her.

Their mouths crashed together. Viera felt the need to have more of Thorn. The desire between them grew. It became more than just her, it felt like it would explode out of her. As Thorn continued to move her hand, the heat boiled within her, taking her over, until stars exploded all around her, and yet it continued.

Thorn's emotions washed over her, around her, through her, she knew her lover was close. "Come for me!" She wasn't sure who said the words.

As fireworks exploded, the world seemed to waver and stretch. She screamed out in pleasure, in delight, in ecstasy. It was too much ... nothing had ever been so perfect. The orgasm rocketed through every pore of her body just before the world went black.

She lay in the bed under the covers and curled into Thorn. Everything felt right. She never wanted to move.

"You finally awake, my fire cloud?"

Viera groaned. "How long did I sleep?"

"You're cute when you're snoring."

"I don't snore!" She ducked under the covers to hide her blush.

"You go on telling yourself that, Ms. Snores-A-Lot." Thorn chuckled.

"I know this is going to sound weird but, did something happen ... you know ... at the end. It felt, I don't know, stretchy, and weird. Really weird. It felt like our ... climax, I dunno, was universal. Does that even make sense?" The heat of Viera's blush was getting worse. She wondered if it reached her waist yet.

"You mean, when we both orgasmed? And then you passed out?"

Viera ducked her head under the covers. "That didn't happen." She knew it sounded insane ... and it *did* happen, but why?

"It was adorable." Thorn pulled her back out and kissed her, soundly. "I've never made a woman pass out with pleasure before. I may have a new standard."

"God above, you're awful." Viera shook her head. "It felt like I was orgasming across the galaxy. I don't know, I mean, you're good, fantastic, but it was ... I just don't know, weird and wonderful, but..." Viera floundered.

"I need to get to the deck. Let's discuss this at lunch. Maybe we can figure it out then." She gave Viera one more kiss and headed to the bathroom to get ready for the day.

After she left, Viera dressed, then followed Thorn. She headed first to grab food, and then to the training room. She sat in the chair and considered the pencil. *Why can't I get you to move? I can't move the air. I can't move the pencil. Water? What is the fourth element? Fuck! I need a book.*

Flower Prancer sauntered in. "Have you made the pencil move?"

"Without my hand?"

His disappointment was palpable. "Yes, Viera. Without your hand."

She smiled wanly at the yonat. "No. I was thinking about the four types of elemental magic. I obviously don't have air, wait, you called it 'gas.' I also don't have a proficiency for solids. That leaves liquids and ... what? You never did tell me the last one."

"It's a catch-all for everything else. Though, largely, it's the manipulation of energy. Most humans have gas and solid. That is why we started there."

She narrowed her eyes at him. "Most other humans, you mean the *five* other humans who can perform magic. All your theories are based on the five pillars?"

"And the pillars before them." She felt his annoyance at being questioned.

"Their parents, grandparents, relatives I assume?"

"Yes," he admitted.

"So, everything you're assuming about my magic is based on hereditary magic from five families. For a crazy moment, can you test me as if you have no base knowledge of my race?" She gave him a 'don't hate me' smile.

Despite the smile, she could feel his exasperation growing. His voice stayed level. "I would like to stick with the plan I've set up."

She blew out a huff of air. "You're the boss."

His irritation turned to an annoyed acceptance. *Why is he teaching me if I can't do anything right?*

"Did you have enough coffee this morning?"

"Yes, but I can always have more."

His tail flicked. "Go, get some coffee and a glass of water."

She sighed. His vexation dropped as she immediately went to do his bidding. When she returned with the mug and glass, she put the glass near the pencil, but kept the mug clasped in her hands, drinking in both the scents as well as the flavor of the morning brew.

"Please try to move the water." There was a level of hope in his words.

She smiled at him and then lowered her coffee to her lap. Viera closed her eyes and imagined the table. *What could I do with water? Make a ball? Have it float? Fly at Flower Prancer? Or the wall? The wall sounds safer. Though, if my eyes are closed, how would he know?*

She smiled and opened her eyes. Nothing on the table had moved. With a growl, she narrowed her eyes, but still, the pencil and water didn't seem at all intimidated.

Before Flower Prancer could react—she *knew* he would swish his tail—she held up her hand. "Just don't."

"Don't what?"

"Your disapproval, your frustration. I need you to help me figure this out without being constantly upset with me." She hadn't meant to snap at him, but she'd spent her life on proper pedagogical sciences, and he wasn't doing it right.

His head tilted. "I haven't said anything negative, Viera. You're commenting on my emotions, not my words."

She lifted her hands and shook her head. "Whatever, I just ... it's too much."

"How many emotions have you been sensing, Earthling?"

"I don't know ... all of them. I've been picking up on emotions for a day or two ... I guess. Why, is it important?" She just wanted to get past the pencil and water.

Flower Prancer stepped forward. "Sensing is one of the non-elemental proficiencies. If you can sense emotions with this level of precision, then I know how to start your training. All we have left is your elemental skill. Viera, tell me, has anything else weird happened in the last few days?"

"I don't know ... everything?"

His exasperation shot up and she sighed. He huffed. "You are sensitive. Tell me everything from when Commander Firoza and I entered the room. Don't leave anything out, even if it seems small and obvious. Assume I know nothing."

She wanted to roll her eyes, but she obliged.

"Stop. Repeat that last bit."

Viera sipped her coffee to stop from screaming. It was the fifth time he'd asked for clarification. "You threatened the guards, told Thorn to meet us back at her unit, and the world turned odd, like we were under water." She sipped her coffee again, waiting for his question. When it didn't come she nodded. "Then you ran ... really fast. You got around all the other beasts, though it looked like we swam with how the world looked."

"Stop."

Viera sighed. This day would never end ... ever!

"Close your eyes."

She did. She felt fully conditioned to not fight an Elder. The dustification of the bug-beast helped.

"Imagine the feeling of how it felt when you were on my back. The underwater feeling. Imagine you're on the other side of a waterfall and people can't see you."

A coolness flowed through her in a smooth wave. Her muscles relaxed as she felt her power vibrate within her. She breathed out as Flower Prancer's approval seeped in.

"Open your eyes, Viera."

She did. At first nothing was different, but then she realized the walls were wavering, as if underwater. "What?"

The yonat moved to the wall. He tapped the wall with his hoof. "Mirror, half wall."

As she watched, half the wall shimmered into a mirror. It took her a moment to shift from being amazed at seeing the transformation of the wall to realizing what she saw in the reflection.

In the center stood the white unicorn with violet eyes and sparkling rainbow mane and tail. Behind him ... a table with a glass of water and a pencil on it.

The rest of the room was empty.

Holy fuck ... I'm invisible!

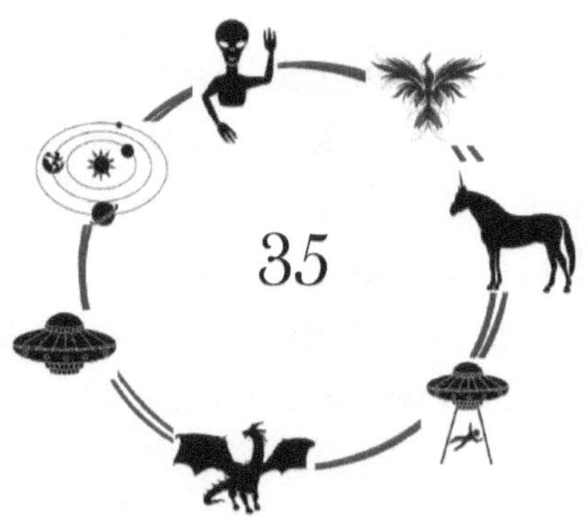

A Scrolling Marquee Is A Thing

Viera

Viera woke up early. She slipped from the bed and padded to the restroom. After her shower and soak, she brushed her straight hair flat, and felt giddy about the thought that they'd probably get home in a few hours.

She narrowed her blue eyes at herself in the mirror and thought *disappear.* Nothing happened. *Okay, what was the analogy? Waterfalls? Portal, Viera! Be on the other side of the stupid waterfall.* She tensed her muscles, trying to activate her magic. Nothing.

She thought about the cool relaxed feeling of the day before and took a deep meditative breath and blew it out. *Invisible.*

Her reflection shimmered and was gone. Viera held her breath. She stopped moving. Gaping, she leaned in closer to see if anything showed up in the mirror.

Not believing her eyes, she slowly raised a hand and waved it in front of her face. Then she waved it faster. Then she did a small jig of glee, a squeal of delight escaping her.

Both hands covering her mouth, she watched where her reflection should be. Outside the mirror, she could see herself fine, including her chest that moved up and down as she breathed fast. *Reveal.*

The cool wave of peace washed through her and her slightly manic face appeared in the mirror. Her smile grew as she danced around the bathroom trying not to make any noise.

Okay, girly, clothes, breakfast, then ... maybe hang with Scout today.

Outside of the bathroom she found Thorn waiting, gazing at her watch. "Done?"

"Oh! Sorry, I thought you were asleep."

Thorn spent a moment slowly taking in her naked body. "It was worth the wait."

Viera blushed. Then her jaw dropped. "Oh! I totally forgot about my watch! I bet it's charged."

Thorn chuckled as she headed into the bathroom. "My guess would be yes. It takes about an hour, and it's been days." The restroom door closed behind her.

In the closet, Viera selected light gray linen pants and a sky-blue doublet. After securing the belt, she checked out the pockets and decided it would hold her phone. In the small charging compartment, she first found her watch, turned it on, and strapped it on her wrist.

Friday, seven a.m.

It was such a small thing, but for some reason it centered her.

Next came her phone. Before she could turn it on, Thorn came out of the restroom looking ready to take on the world. Viera waved her phone. "This is hilarious. It isn't like I'll be able to use it before we get to Earth, yet I'm so excited to have it back."

"What do you mean you can't use it?"

"Are you telling me you have Wi-Fi on this ship? A cell tower?" Amusement bubbled in her at the thought of a tall pole sticking up from the top ... bottom? ... of the Ziner covered with cellular dish receivers.

Viera could feel Thorn's amusement. "Do you want to know all the technicalities?"

"Um, probably not?"

"Because I'm sure Horax will be happy to explain them to you. But, yes, your phone will work." She winked.

Viera landed on the bed. "Oh. Well. I guess I know what I'll be doing this morning. What will I tell my friends and family? I'm guessing some of them have called and texted."

"Just remember, there aren't a lot of truths you can share. Maybe write up a few details so you know what you want to tell everyone before you contact your friends and family?" She leaned down and gave Viera a kiss before heading out.

She gazed down at her phone. It suddenly occurred to her that the previous week felt like a dream, living in a sci-fi or fantasy novel, and once she turned on her phone, she would be waking up, returning to her life. *Do I want to return? Once this is over I'm back to being me. Teach, alone, no Thorn.* She gulped down any disappointment, refusing to think about that. Viera took a moment to close her eyes and settle. *It'll be fine. It isn't like Thorn will be out of my life.*

With a sigh, she pressed the button and watched as the screen flash to life. The time and date appeared as well as an image of a cat romping through a field of Monet's flowers.

Then like a ticker screen, notification started scrolling up her phone. Her eyes glazed as she picked out the names of the people who'd called and texted.

Fuck! I need to call Betsy before she sends every governmental service out looking for me!

Viera's stomach grumbled. She opened her phone and rubbed her eyes, deciding to read the texts after breakfast.

Hi, Betsy, she typed out. *I went up north to a cabin without service. Didn't realize until now. Sorry! We can talk when I get home.*

Her phone dinged instantly. *Finally! Call me, now!*

Viera massaged her temples. *I need coffee. I'll be home sometime this afternoon. Let's talk then.*

She could imagine her friend's snarl, even from space this far away. *Fine, but we need to discuss this disappearing act, Viera!*

Huffing out a large breath of air, Viera closed her phone and pocketed it. In the mess hall, she went to the kitchen and asked for eggs, sausage, and pancakes with a side of coffee. She couldn't order it on a panel, but there were people she could ask who helped her.

She found a table in the corner and read through a week of more and more frantic texts from Betsy. Guilt weighing her down, Viera drooped as she finished her coffee.

How could I have not thought of the people back home this week?

Metaphorically pulling up her big girl undies, she navigated to her mom's texts. There were fewer. Saturday morning: *If you didn't want to go out with Donald, you could've just told me. No reason to stand him up.*

Sunday: *Viera, why aren't you texting me back? Was there something wrong with this guy? What aren't you telling me?*

Tuesday: *Should I be worried? You never go this long. Text me.*

Wednesday: *I need you to get back to me, dear. Whatever is wrong, we can fix it.*

There weren't more texts, but Viera found several voice messages from both Betsy and her mom. She sighed. *Back to life ... back to reality.*

She sent a text to her mom, repeating the excuse she gave Betsy.

Oh thank goodness! You're talking to me. I'll stop with the dates if that's what made you so upset, dear.

It wasn't that. However, she wasn't upset with the outcome. *I love you, Mom. I'm still not home. Can we talk tomorrow?*

Her mom took a bit longer to respond. *Of course, dear.*

With a groan, Viera trudged to where the food was prepared. "Another coffee please."

Back at the table, she dove into her emails.

36

Home ... And It's Still Not Kansas

Viera

"Hi, Ms. Kor!" Scout dropped down at her table with a plate of pancakes.

"Hi, kiddo. How are you?" Viera closed her phone, ready to be back on the ship and away from Earth for a few minutes.

"Great! Mom said you should return to pack. We should be back to Earth soon." He dug into his food.

"What about you? You'll be all alone."

"No, I won't, I have Beaver!" She laughed at his enthusiasm.

She leaned over and gave Scout a quick hug. "Enjoy your meal. Eat something that isn't sugar."

He giggled as she headed out.

Back in the room she shared with Thorn, she found the suitcase in the bottom of the closet. As she folded all of the clothes into the bag, Thorn entered. "Good, you're here! I didn't want you to leave all your stuff behind again."

"No, I learned my lesson last time."

Thorn came over and wrapped her in a hug, dipping her head for a quick kiss. "I'm going to miss having you share my space."

Viera smiled. "I agree, but you're going to be my student's mom in a few days, Ms. Firoza."

Thorn bit her lower lip. "We'll see. I may have to ignore that."

"Hmm," Viera rubbed against Thorn's body. "Maybe."

They moved apart before things got too heated. "You know," Viera said, "I'm a bit disappointed I missed going through the GPS. It was so interesting last time."

Thorn laughed. "I think you know when we went through the portal."

"What are you talking about?"

Viera continued to pack as Thorn watched her. "You told me your type of magic is a sensitivity to the things around you, right?"

"Yes, I think. It isn't that clear. I really wish there was a book I could read. Maybe one of the pillars can help me with that. Do you know who they are? Can you introduce me?"

"Yeah, I can get you in touch with one back on Earth, that won't be a problem. But focus, Viera. Remember your 'intergalactic' orgasm?"

The heat rushed up her face and she covered it up with both her hands. "Oh, my God, stop! I told you it was nothing."

"Yeah, a nothing that caused you to pass out, it was so good." Thorn smirked. "We're going to have to see if we can replicate that, by the way. I like being so good you lose consciousness. It's an ego stroke."

Viera scrunched up her face behind her hands and shook her head. "Okay, enough. I felt the trip through the GPS. Got it. Now, back to packing."

Thorn came up behind her and wrapped her arms around her. She kissed the top of Viera's head. "So, you'll consider spending more time with me back on Earth? Dating, accidently leaving clothes at my house, extra tutoring sessions with Scout?"

Viera leaned back into Thorn. Everything in her wanted to scream 'yes!' She finally dropped her hands and turned, then wrapped Thorn in an embrace. "I'd like that."

They kissed, and Viera lost track of time as she traced her hands up and curled her fingers in Thorn's hair. She began to feel it didn't matter where they stood; as long as they were together, she'd be home.

Danger, Viera, danger. This is a short-term dalliance, you know that. It was how this started. You won't live nearly as long as this lovely alien in front of you.

Once they broke apart, she smiled, but it was a bit sad. Thorn was already back to organizing her stuff and didn't notice.

It didn't take long to finish packing up her stuff. Though she and Scout were beamed into his room, there was a platform that was an easier staging area for transport. Being the guest, Viera would be the first sent down to Earth. She gave Thorn and Scout a hug and gave Beaver a quick pet.

Viera turned to Horax. "I can't believe I got to meet a real dragon ... or rather a qynad. You're the best Horax." She leaned in to hug his neck. "I'm going to miss learning everything from you." She felt herself getting misty.

"Oh, I don't think this is the last you'll see or hear from me, young pillar. I'm sure we'll have many more conversations. You're too good of a student." He winked. "Especially for a teacher."

After saying her good-byes to Horax and the other crew members she'd met, she then stepped up to the platform. *Beam me down, Horax.*

The ship dissolved, melting around her, replaced with her living room. Instead of facing her TV, a furious Betsy faced her.

Holy shit!

Betsy pointed an accusatory finger at her, then up at her ceiling. Then the finger came back down to point at Viera's chest. Her face a mask of fury, Betsy snarled, "Where the fuck did they take you?"

Thank you for reading!

Galaxy Lessons

Please Leave a review for this book so others know how much you enjoyed reading it.

Find more information on my <u>books on my website</u>

Acknowledgement

I was on a reading page where readers were asking for different types of books. Someone asked for a book that combined the science fiction of space and aliens with fun fantasy aspects found in good urban fantasy. I realized I hadn't seen many books like this.

Later, when I was looking for the specific subtitle, it was my son who said he'd heard of space fantasy. It wasn't something I was terribly familiar with because I tend more towards urban fantasy. Anyway, at the end of the day, I had a ton of fun writing this book and the others in this series.

As always, I want to thank the wonderful team of people that guarantee my words are whipped into shape. Angela Grimes and Weslee Imrisek are the best editors a writer could ask for. Nikki and Nita are wonderful alpha readers, encouraging me and amusing me every step of the way. And as always my son who lets me bombard him with my ideas and then helps me refine them.

About the Author

Harlowe Frost has been a teacher at both the high school and college level. Her parents instilled a love of reading from a young age. She grew up in the queer community. Her favorite genre growing up was fantasy and science fiction, that is, until she discovered urban fantasy and paranormal romance. What she never found in those books was the diversity in background, gender identity, and sexuality she saw in the people around her. She decided if she couldn't find that in what she read, then she would write it herself. This started her writing paranormal romance with a LGBTQ+ background.

www.ingramcontent.com/pod-product-compliance
Lightning Source LLC
Chambersburg PA
CBHW032245310726
48973CB00008B/2300